"A baby was left in my care and it's possible that you're the father."

Keely hadn't intended to blurt it out like that, but she had a job to do. Expect now she felt bad. The poor guy was so shocked, the color drained from his face.

"Mine? You've got to be kidding," Devon replied.

"I'm not, believe me. This isn't something I would joke about."

He shook his head, staring at the floor, obviously trying to grip the announcement. While Keely waited for him to speak again, several emotions passed across his face.

Then his jaw clenched a few times and his gaze returned to Keely. "Did you say this baby *could* be mine? Does that mean he might not be?"

"He could be yours or he could belong to another man," she said quietly.

"Of course," he said caustically.

The relief in his voice worried Keely, as did her attraction to this man she'd only just laid eyes on.

Which left her to wonder, what had she gotten herself into?

Dear Reader,

Welcome to more juicy reads from Silhouette Special Edition. I'd like to highlight Silhouette veteran and RITA® Award finalist Teresa Hill, who has written over ten Silhouette books under the pseudonym Sally Tyler Hayes. Her second story for us, *Heard It Through the Grapevine,* has all the ingredients for a fast-paced read—marriage of convenience, a pregnant preacher's daughter and a handsome hero to save the day. Teresa Hill writes, "I love this heroine because she takes a tremendous leap of faith. She hopes that her love will break down the hero's walls, and she never holds back." Don't miss this touching story!

USA TODAY bestselling and award-winning author Susan Mallery returns to her popular miniseries HOMETOWN HEARTBREAKERS with *One in a Million.* Here, a sassy single mom falls for a drop-dead-gorgeous FBI agent, but sets a few ground rules—a little romance, no strings attached. Of course, we know rules are meant to be broken! Victoria Pade delights us with *The Baby Surprise,* the last in her BABY TIMES THREE miniseries, in which a confirmed bachelor discovers he may be a father. With encouragement from a beautiful heroine, he feels ready to be a parent…and a husband.

The next book in Laurie Paige's SEVEN DEVILS miniseries, *The One and Only* features a desirable medical assistant with a secret past who snags the attention of a very charming doctor. Judith Lyons brings us *Alaskan Nights,* which involves two opposites who find each other irritating, yet totally irresistible! Can these two survive a little engine trouble in the wilderness? In *A Mother's Secret,* Pat Warren tells of a mother in search of her secret child and the discovery of the man of her dreams.

This month is all about love against the odds and finding that special someone when you least expect it. As you lounge in your favorite chair, lose yourself in one of these gems!

Sincerely,

Karen Taylor Richman
Senior Editor

Please address questions and book requests to:
Silhouette Reader Service
U.S.: 3010 Walden Ave., P.O. Box 1325, Buffalo, NY 14269
Canadian: P.O. Box 609, Fort Erie, Ont. L2A 5X3

The Baby Surprise

VICTORIA PADE

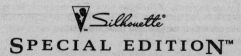

SPECIAL EDITION™

Published by Silhouette Books

America's Publisher of Contemporary Romance

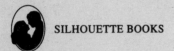 SILHOUETTE BOOKS

ISBN 0-373-24544-0

THE BABY SURPRISE

Copyright © 2003 by Victoria Pade

This edition published by arrangement with Harlequin Books S.A.

® and TM are trademarks of Harlequin Books S.A., used under license.
Trademarks indicated with ® are registered in the United States Patent
and Trademark Office, the Canadian Trade Marks Office and in other
countries.

Visit Silhouette at www.eHarlequin.com

Printed in U.S.A.

Books by Victoria Pade

Silhouette Special Edition

Breaking Every Rule #402
Divine Decadence #473
Shades and Shadows #502
Shelter from the Storm #527
Twice Shy #558
Something Special #600
Out on a Limb #629
The Right Time #689
Over Easy #710
Amazing Gracie #752
Hello Again #778
Unmarried with Children #852
*Cowboy's Kin #923
*Baby My Baby #946
*Cowboy's Kiss #970

*A Ranching Family
†Baby Times Three

Mom for Hire #1057
*Cowboy's Lady #1106
*Cowboy's Love #1159
*The Cowboy's Ideal Wife #1185
*Baby Love #1249
*Cowboy's Caress #1311
*The Cowboy's Gift-Wrapped
 Bride #1365
*Cowboy's Baby #1389
*Baby Be Mine #1431
*On Pins and Needles #1443
Willow in Bloom #1490
†Her Baby Secret #1503
†Maybe My Baby #1515
†The Baby Surprise #1544

Silhouette Books

World's Most Eligible Bachelors
Wyoming Wrangler

Montana Mavericks:
 Wed in Whitehorn
The Marriage Bargain

The Coltons
From Boss to Bridegroom

VICTORIA PADE

is a bestselling author of both historical and contemporary romance fiction, and the mother of two energetic daughters, Cori and Erin. Although she enjoys her chosen career as a novelist, she occasionally laments that she has never traveled farther from her Colorado home than Disneyland; instead she spends all her spare time plugging away at her computer. She takes breaks from writing by indulging in her favorite hobby—eating chocolate.

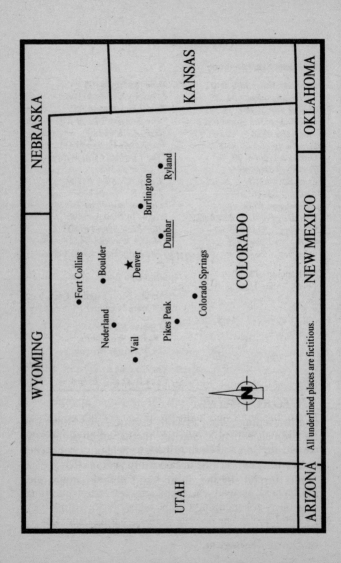

WYOMING

NEBRASKA

KANSAS

UTAH

• Fort Collins

Nederland •

• Boulder

★ Denver

Vail •

Pikes Peak •

Colorado Springs

COLORADO

Dunbar

Burlington •

Ryland

OKLAHOMA

ARIZONA   All underlined places are fictitious.

NEW MEXICO

Chapter One

Keely Gilhooley found the address she was looking
for and pulled her conservative sedan up to the curb
in front of the house.

The circa 1940s modest red-brick two-story was
trimmed in white and surrounded by a covered porch
that was bordered halfway up by brick.

Keely couldn't tell from the street if anyone was
home, but since she hadn't found any other addresses
for the renowned freelance wildlife photographer who
owned the place, she didn't know where else to con-
nect with him on a Monday afternoon.

She turned off the engine and checked the computer printout on the passenger seat.

Eighteen thirty-four—that was the number on the
paper, that was the number on the house. The home
of Devon Tarlington.

Keely sighed, resigned to what she had to do but not liking it. How could anyone like being put in an uncomfortably awkward position against her will?

She was used to locating people—that was her job. She and her sister Hillary ran Where Are They Now?, an organization that specialized in tracing people, mostly via the Internet. But once they'd done that, they turned the information over to their client and it was up to the client to contact or confront the person. This was the first time Keely had had both to find someone and face him. And with news she certainly didn't want to deliver.

But there was no other choice. She and Hillary had been left holding the bag—in a manner of speaking. And then Keely had lost the coin toss with Hillary that determined which of them had to meet Devon Tarlington. So it was up to her.

''Ready or not, here I come,'' she announced, getting out of the car and heading up the walk.

On the way she kept an eye on the enormous picture window to the right of the front door. But still she couldn't tell if, on the other side of it, someone was watching her approach.

There were five cement steps to take her onto the porch and as she trudged up them she was wondering what kind of reception she would have if Devon Tarlington *was* home. She was wondering what kind of person he was. Would he be some big, hulking, scary guy who might not separate the message from the messenger? Who might blow up at her?

The porch didn't have any furniture on it. No warm

wicker. No slatted chair swinging from chains. No flowerpots. Not even a welcome mat to give her hope that he might be a friendly sort. It *was* October in Colorado and those things could all have been put away for the winter, she reasoned. Plus, on the positive side, there wasn't a huge, grizzly-toothed dog or an Approach At Your Own Risk sign, either.

But still she was wary.

As she went up to the front door she caught a glimpse of herself reflected in the oval of beveled glass that filled the center of the top half of the oak panel. She took a quick assessment of her appearance, trying to see if she could give herself a don't-even-think-about-messing-with-me air to protect herself in case Devon Tarlington didn't take kindly to what he was about to find out.

Her long, curly red hair had been even more riotous than usual this morning so she'd had to pull it into a scrunchie at her crown. That seemed like a mistake now. How tough was a scrunchie, after all?

She had on jeans and a red turtleneck, and that was okay. No frills or fluff. No nonsense. But she *had* applied a little mascara and blusher, so she practiced narrowing her green eyes to look intimidating if the need arose.

It didn't help. She doubted she could convince anyone she was a brute of a woman. She just had to hope she didn't need to be.

In any event, she squared her shoulders to at least appear stronger and braver than she felt, and rang the doorbell.

She didn't have to wait long before the door opened and when it did she was slightly taken aback at her first glimpse of the man standing on the other side. Not because he was frightening. He was just that good-looking.

He was tall—over six feet to her five foot five—and extremely well built, with long legs, a narrow waist and hips, and shoulders and pectorals that seemed to go on forever. And all of it was attached to a dream of a face that was angular and sharp-edged, with deep-set blue eyes the color of new denim, a straight nose, agile lips with just a hint of a sardonic upturn to their corners, and dark brown hair that was cut short and left slightly mussed on top.

"Can I help you?" he asked when she just stood there gawking instead of introducing herself.

It took Keely a moment to realize she was staring and not speaking. Finally she yanked her wits back in order and said, "I'm looking for Devon Tarlington."

Now why had her voice come out sounding like a lame-duck freshman addressing the senior captain of the football team who also happened to be the class president voted most hunky boy in the school?

And it didn't help when those nimble lips eased into a sexy, sexy half smile. Or when, in a second taste of deep, rich baritone, he said, "That's me."

Keely reminded herself why she was there, drew herself up a second time, put on her most professional face and said, "My name is Keely Gilhooley—"

He laughed.

The jerk had the nerve to laugh at her name.

"Keely Gilhooley?" he repeated. "And with that flaming red hair? You wouldn't happen to be a little Irish, would you?"

"A little," she said facetiously, trying to maintain her pique when his half smile turned into an endearing grin and he stretched a long arm up the edge of the door, shifting his weight more to one hip than the other with an innate sensuality.

"It's great hair, by the way," he said then, not like a come-on but as if he genuinely liked her hair. Which put power to the compliment.

But again Keely reminded herself that this was not some kind of social event and that, considering what she'd come to tell this man, he was about the last guy on earth she would want anything to do with even if he *was* traffic-stoppingly handsome and disarmingly charming.

"May I come in?" she asked.

"I don't know. Why do you want to?" he countered.

Keely took out one of her business cards and handed it to him.

He took it and read from it. "Where Are They Now?"

"We're a people-locating service," Keely informed him.

"Is somebody looking for me or are you just going door-to-door to drum up business?"

"Someone is looking for you."

"Who?"

"Well, actually, me. But it would be better if we talked inside, in private."

The grin reappeared. "You're who's looking for me and you want privacy?"

Keely ignored the insinuation—and the fact that he seemed to be enjoying himself so much. "Yes, I'm who's looking for you. Sort of. And it's privacy I think *you'll* want for what I have to tell you."

Slightly full eyebrows arched, but only in mock wariness. "That sounds ominous. Or maybe it's just supposed to so I'll let you inside and then you'll hit me over the head and have your way with me."

The idea of having her way with him lit a bit of a spark somewhere in the recesses of Keely. But she ignored it. "Could we just go inside and talk?"

"Is it something I'm going to want to hear?"

"I don't know you, so I really couldn't say."

"It must not be that I've won a million dollars or something."

"No, it isn't that you've won a million dollars."

"And you don't know if it's something I'll think is bad or not?"

"No, I don't know that."

"But it could be that I'll think it's good?"

He was toying with her and already she knew that Devon Tarlington was incorrigible.

And she was also already wishing that that obvious streak of bad boy wasn't so appealing.

But once more she fought to rise above that appeal.

"Do you want to know what I have to tell you or not?" she said, bluffing because there was no way she was leaving here *without* telling him what she'd come to tell him.

"Let's see..." He pretended to think about it, studying her face the entire time and—to his credit—not once letting those denim-blue eyes drop below her chin. "A fiery redhead shows up at my door unannounced and wants a secret meeting with me to tell me something important enough for her to have put effort into finding me...."

"I don't need a *secret* meeting with you. Just a private one," she amended.

But the amendment didn't seem to matter to him because he went on scrutinizing her a moment longer before he pushed off the door and said, "Okay. I can't resist." Then he swept an arm in belated invitation and tacked on, "Please, come in."

Finally, Keely thought as she stepped into his entryway, waiting near the staircase directly ahead of the door while he closed it and turned to face her.

"Would the living room be private enough?" he asked with a poke of his sculpted chin in that direction.

"I think so," she said, preceding him when he waited for her to.

The room that went with the picture window had clearly been decorated without a woman's touch. There weren't any knickknacks or plants or pictures on the walls. There was only a large brown leather sofa and matching overstuffed chair, a coffee table littered with remote controls and TV listings, and an entertainment center complete with big-screen television, VCR, DVD player and an array of stereo equipment that Keely thought she'd need a six-month training course to operate.

"Have a seat, Keely Gilhooley," he suggested.

Keely ignored the teasing repetition of her name and chose the overstuffed chair to sit on while he perched on the closest arm of the sofa, angled in her direction.

"Now, tell me why you 'sort of' came looking for me," he said, using the words she'd said to him.

"I *was* looking for you, but not on my own behalf," she qualified.

"And on whose behalf were you looking for me?" he asked as if this were all nothing more than an amusement to break up an afternoon.

"On behalf of Clarissa Coburn."

Devon Tarlington didn't find *that* name so amusing. His face sobered into a full-out scowl and his blue eyes clouded with instant anger.

"Clarissa Coburn and I have nothing to say to each other," he said flatly, definitively, devoid of any of the warmth that had been in his voice a split second earlier.

"I'm afraid it isn't that simple," Keely said. She was no longer worried that Devon Tarlington might be the kind of man who would strike out at her. She could tell he wasn't. But that still didn't make what she had to say any easier.

"It seems pretty simple to me," he said. "Clarissa Coburn is history and there isn't anything—*anything*—to do with her that I'm interested in."

"She has a son," Keely said, dropping the bomb to halt what she could see was about to turn into her eviction. "An eight-month-old baby. Harley. And he could be yours."

She felt bad. The poor guy was so shocked the color drained from his face.

But he rebounded in a hurry and, in a louder voice, said, "Mine? You have to be kidding."

"I'm not, believe me. This isn't something I would joke about."

He shook his head, staring at the floor now rather than at her as if he were replaying something in his mind or trying to get a grip on her announcement. In the process, several things flashed across his expression. Disgust. Disbelief. Denial—or at least the urge to deny. Finally, what looked like anger.

His jaw clenched a few times and his gaze returned to Keely. "Did you say this baby *could* be mine? Does that mean he might *not* be?"

The next part was even harder to say. "He could be yours or he could belong to a man named Brian Rooney," she said quietly.

But for some reason that didn't come as the additional shock she'd thought it would. It almost seemed to relieve him somewhat.

"Of course," he said caustically.

So he'd already known there had been someone else with Clarissa at the same time he was with her. Keely had wondered.

But then it registered that the reason he was relieved by that fact was because he hoped Harley was the other man's child and she couldn't help feeling protective of the baby who was now in her charge.

She tamped down on that, though, just as she kept having to tamp down on noticing how amazingly handsome Devon Tarlington was. Her own emotions were not relevant in this. She was merely the outsider facilitating what needed to happen from here on.

With that in mind, she continued. "Clarissa has disappeared and left Harley behind. But not before arranging with a lawyer to have custody of him relinquished to his father. As soon as it's determined which of you *is* his father."

That seemed to dissolve whatever small amount of relief Devon Tarlington felt, and every remarkable angle, every chiseled plane of his face tensed all over again.

"So she's bailed on her own baby, too," he said through a tight jaw.

"Yes."

"Where is he?"

That simple question and the concern it showed went a long way in redeeming him.

"Harley is with my sister Hillary. Clarissa had us appointed his temporary guardians until paternity is established and then we're to turn him over to his father. He's a great baby, though. Adorable. Even-tempered. As sweet as he can be...."

Okay, she was letting her own emotions rise to the surface again. She had to stop that.

"I'm sure you'll like him," she finished feebly.

"Clarissa didn't have any idea which of us is the father?"

"None."

Devon Tarlington's expression was still like a storm cloud and Keely knew she'd tapped into something that was deep and dark for him. But she had to admire the control he was exhibiting. And she appreciated that he didn't seem to be confusing the message with the messenger the way she'd been afraid he might.

Still, for another long moment, he didn't speak. He stared off into the distance, pensively, apparently working to absorb this turn of events.

Then he said, "So what now?"

"You were easy to locate. But I haven't found Brian Rooney yet."

Devon's jaw pulsed yet again. Then, in a stilted voice, he said, "Both Brian and I are from a small town out on the eastern plains—Dunbar. You might start looking there. That's where his family is and they're bound to know something about him."

So the two men knew each other. They were even from the same place. A small town. Had they merely been acquainted with each other, or had they been friends? Keely wondered.

But she didn't pry.

"Is there any chance Brian knew Clarissa was pregnant?" Devon asked then.

"Clarissa said in the letter she left-that neither of you knew. Which means that once I locate this other man I'll have to go to him in person because I don't think it's news that should be given over the telephone, especially by a stranger. Plus I'll need to get some blood from him for typing and DNA comparison—if the blood type alone isn't conclusive. So really, I'm at the very beginning of this.''

"You'll need blood from me, too, then, right?''

"Right.''

Devon Tarlington shook his head again, his disgust blatant now. "I can't believe this.''

"I know it's a lot to digest,'' Keely said softly. "But honestly, it isn't a joke.''

"Yeah, at the end Clarissa wasn't quite as many laughs as she started out to be,'' he said wryly, more to himself than to her. "So what do you want me to do? Go to my doctor or what?''

"I've made arrangements with an independent lab to do the testing. You'll need to go in to have blood drawn. I haven't taken Harley in yet, but I will, and then the three samples will be looked at for a match,'' she explained.

"Are you sure there's only two possibilities?'' he asked then.

"For who could be Harley's father? I'm just relaying what I've been told—Harley's dad is either you or Brian Rooney.''

Devon Tarlington nodded, then shook his head yet again, clearly having trouble believing this.

But in spite of that he said, "I can't go to the lab tomorrow, I have a business meeting that'll take most of the day. How about Wednesday?''

"Okay.'' She was grateful that he wasn't putting

up more of a fuss. She had been worried that he might refuse and she hadn't had a contingency plan if he did.

"And the baby—did you say he's with you and your sister now?"

"Yes. We share a house and he's staying with us."

"Is that all right with you and your sister?"

Again his concern for someone other than himself earned him points with her. "My sister and I are crazy about him, so yes, it's okay that he's with us."

Devon Tarlington seemed to hesitate then and whatever was going through his mind must have disturbed him because the frown lines were back between his brows before he said, "Maybe I should meet him."

"It probably wouldn't do any harm," Keely agreed.

He sighed once more, obviously struggling fiercely with the possibility of fatherhood. "How about tomorrow? In the evening?" he suggested.

"That would be fine," she answered, working to fight the slight eruption of excitement she felt at the prospect of seeing this man again herself, an excitement she knew she had no business feeling.

And since she didn't really have anything else to say to him, she stood to go. "Thank you for not hitting the ceiling," she said as she did.

Devon Tarlington stood, too, and walked her back to the front door. "I couldn't very well hit the ceiling with you. You didn't have anything to do with this, did you?" he asked with a hint of that smile that he'd flashed so easily before he knew what she was there to tell him.

"No, I just wasn't sure what kind of a reaction I might find. I didn't think this would be particularly welcome news."

"Yeah, it probably would have been better to hear that Miss Keely Irish-Eyes Gilhooley had looked me up for something a little more tantalizing," he agreed in a deep, devilish tone that let her know he'd returned to the teasing he'd greeted her with, albeit more subdued. "But it was nice to meet you anyway."

"You, too," she countered, still trying to hide just how nice it was.

"I'll probably need your address for tomorrow night," he said then, as if it had just occurred to him.

"Oh. Yes, you probably will need that."

She took another of her business cards out of her purse, wrote her address on the back and handed it to him, watching as he read it simply because she couldn't take her eyes off him.

"This is close by," he said when he glanced from the card to her again.

"It took me about ten minutes to get here."

"So all this time you've been right under my nose and I didn't even know you were there."

"Well, not *right* under your nose, but not too far from here. About six blocks."

"Strange to think of that," he mused for no reason she understood.

So, rather than commenting on it, she said, "Then I guess I'll see you tomorrow evening."

"Bet on it," he answered decisively as she said goodbye and left him standing in the doorway.

And as she returned to her car, Keely wondered if he'd forgotten that he was coming to her place to meet his potential son rather than to see her.

But it gave her a dangerous little thrill just the same.

Chapter Two

Clarissa Coburn.

That was a name Devon had hoped never to hear again. And by the next morning, as he went through photographs he'd taken of wild boars in Africa in preparation for his meeting with a gallery owner, he still wasn't happy that he'd had to.

He considered Clarissa—hands down—the biggest mistake of his life. A mistake he'd already paid dearly for. And now he had to wonder if it was going to haunt him forever.

She'd seemed so perfect for him when he'd met her at a bar in Denver. Dancing on a table, she'd caught his eye immediately, and then she'd literally fallen into his lap and asked him out to dinner.

He'd accepted, of course, pleased by his good fortune and flattered by her initiative. He'd liked her. She was beautiful—tall and leggy, well built, blond, sexy as hell. Not to mention smart and witty and a natural flirt who sucked him in before he even knew she was flirting with him.

Over dinner they'd discovered that they were both free spirits, ready to pack up at a moment's notice and take off—Devon for work, Clarissa for any reason. To Kenya. To Alaska. To east Asia—they'd both been to some of the farthest reaches of the globe and intended to see even more of it.

They'd found that they shared the same likes and dislikes in food, in music, in movies. They even had similar plans for the future—neither of them were interested in marriage or family until much later in life.

They'd just plain hit it off, which had led to them spending the next three months together.

Three wild months during which Devon hadn't thought about anything but Clarissa. Three months during which he hadn't cared if anyone else in the world existed.

Three months during which Clarissa hadn't thought about anyone but Clarissa, or cared if anyone but Clarissa existed, too.

Because that was also Clarissa.

She was a hedonist—that's what she'd said about herself. And she'd proved it again and again. If she wanted something, she made sure she got it. If a whim struck her, she followed it. And whatever felt good to her at any given moment was what she did.

Who cared about the consequences? That was something else she'd said more often than he could count. If there were consequences she didn't like, she just didn't accept them. Or she let someone else deal with them....

"Apparently even if the consequence was a baby," Devon muttered to himself as he began to put the pictures he'd chosen into his portfolio.

An eight-month-old baby.

An eight-month-old baby who could be his....

That possibility hadn't even begun to seem real to Devon yet.

A *baby*...

He could be a *father*....

That might be all right for his older brothers. They'd both only recently become dads under unusual circumstances.

"But me?" Devon said.

He didn't even want to think about it. About what it could mean. About how unsuited he was for parenthood.

He didn't know the first thing about babies or kids or being a father. He wasn't domestic—he paid a service to take care of his yard. He employed a neighbor woman to clean his house and do his laundry, to stock his refrigerator if he was going to be around long enough to actually drink milk.

And that was the biggest thing—his being around. He wasn't. He traveled. A lot. Some months—hell, some *years*—he was away from home more days than he was there. He didn't subscribe to a newspaper because he was never around to read it. He didn't bother with a hardwired telephone or with cable TV because they were a waste of money when he wasn't there to use them.

Did that sound like the description of someone who should be a father?

Of course it didn't.

Plus, he didn't *want* to be a dad. To be the one person some little kid depended on. For everything. For every mouthful of food. For clean diapers and whatever else babies required that he couldn't begin to fathom. For clothes and shelter and learning to walk and talk—how was he supposed to know how to teach someone to walk and talk?

And the kid wouldn't be a baby forever. Then what? Then he'd be the person to teach it right from wrong. The person who had to decide if the kid needed braces and how long to spend on homework and when to let it drive or date or a million other things that parents did.

"Maybe it won't be mine," Devon suggested, realizing he was breaking out in a sweat just thinking about what it would entail if Clarissa's baby was his.

He flipped to the beginning of his portfolio to make sure he had all the photographs in the sequence he wanted them, escaping his own thoughts for a moment.

But only for a moment before the whole subject of a baby, of his own possible parenthood, sneaked back into his mind again.

But it was no easier to believe.

Keely Gilhooley had said it—*he*—was a good baby,

Devon reminded himself as if that might help ease some of the gut-wrenching tension he was experiencing. She'd said Harley was adorable and even-tempered and sweet.

Maybe a little like Keely Gilhooley herself, he thought.

Not that Devon knew anything about her temper or her temperament. But she was pretty adorable.

He'd opened his door to find her on his porch and thought, Well, this is my lucky day.

Little had he known....

But still, Keely Gilhooley—just her name made him smile—was very, very easy to look at. In fact, she was so flawless that, with the autumn sun setting her aglow, for a moment Devon had thought she was some kind of vision.

He had a weakness for redheads. And she was most certainly that. Not just strawberry blond and not the unflattering orangey-red that some people sported. Keely Gilhooley's hair was deep, rich, glistening red. Cherrywood red. And as if that weren't enough, it was full and curly, too. The kind of hair that just made him want to grab handfuls of it as if it was a whole bunch of spun silk.

But the hair was only the beginning of her appeal. She had mesmerizing eyes. Great big, round eyes that were green but so light a green they were luminous. Ethereal eyes that might have made him think she were heaven-sent even without the sun making a halo around her.

And if the hair and eyes weren't enough, she also

had skin like a porcelain doll's. Smooth, perfect radiant skin.

Even her nose was cute—small, narrow, straight— and her lips were pink and full enough not to need lipstick.

Plus her body was nothing to ignore, either. Not too skinny. Not too plump. Firm and compact, with just the right amount up front and in back.

Oh yeah, Keely Gilhooley was something.

"Not that it makes any difference," he said as he judged his portfolio ready and closed it.

Sure, Keely Gilhooley was great-looking and he'd liked her on sight, but he also knew her type. The same type that had gotten him into trouble on the rebound from Clarissa.

He would bet money that Keely Gilhooley was like Patty Hanson—the woman he'd rebounded with after Clarissa. A hometown kind of girl. Wholesome and homespun. A nice, quiet, sedate woman who probably wanted to settle down. Who wanted a husband with a nine-to-five job. A husband who came home to dinner every evening. Who puttered around the house on the weekends and took her to the movies on Saturday night.

There was nothing wrong with that. It was just that Devon considered himself barely housebroken. And he sure as hell wasn't a nine-to-fiver who puttered around the house on weekends.

So, regardless of how appealing Miss Keely Gilhooley was, he knew better than to do more than appreciate her from afar.

"But you certainly did improve the scenery while you were here," he said as if Keely could hear him.

It was true, she *had* improved the scenery and eased the blow of the earth-rocking news she'd delivered.

That he could be a dad...

Devon's stomach clenched anew as that possibility brought him up short again all of a sudden.

He could be a dad, and, tonight, for the first time, he was going to see the child who might have brought that about. The baby he might end up having to raise.

It was a daunting thought.

Almost more than he could handle.

And only one thing kept him from totally freaking out at the prospect of the evening to come—the fact that he was also going to see Keely Gilhooley again.

All right, so that wasn't in keeping with his appreciate-her-from-afar decision.

But still, he was pretty shaken by this turn of events and for now he needed all the incentive he could get to take the next step.

"Is that you, Hill?" Keely called from the bedroom when she heard the front door open.

"It's me," her sister called back.

It was nearly seven-thirty in the evening; Keely had given Harley his bath and was getting him ready for bed while he happily chewed on a clean tennis sock he'd adopted as a teething ring.

After coming up the stairs, Hillary appeared at the doorway and took the extra two steps to the changing table to greet Harley with a rub of the tip of her nose to the tip of his. "Hello, sweet baby."

Harley gave her a slobbery smile for her trouble and she returned to the doorway to lean against the jamb.

Apparently only then did she actually take in Keely.

"Well, look at you!" she said.

Keely was hoping her sister wouldn't notice that she'd primped a little in anticipation of Devon Tarlington's visit. As it was, she'd done it almost against her own will—certainly it had been against her better judgment—and she didn't want to talk about it. So she played dumb. "Look at me? Look at you—you're all dusty and dirty and smudged. And I think you have cobwebs in your hair."

Hillary brushed at the reddish-blond hair she wore very short and spiked on top, and slapped at her sweatshirt.

Other than the hair, the two of them resembled each other so much that they were often mistaken for twins. But Hillary was almost a year younger.

"Are they gone?" she asked, leaning over so Keely could see the top of her head.

"All clear. What were you packing that got you so grimy?" Keely asked, to continue the distraction.

"We had to get some of Brad's stuff out of the attic over there."

"Over there" was the house where Hillary's soon-to-be-husband lived. But since Brad had sold the house, he and Hillary were in the process of moving him into Hillary's and Keely's place in advance of their wedding in two weeks.

"It seems like you should be just about finished, shouldn't you?" Keely said.

"Close," Hillary answered. But rather than offering more than that, she returned to the subject Keely had been trying to avoid. "So, are you having company tonight?"

"Why? Just because my hair is down?"

"And your face is all fresh and you have on *my* kiss-me lipstick and the sweater set I wore the night I got engaged and the jeans that make your butt look good. I don't think I've seen you so fixed up since your divorce."

"I didn't know I've looked so bad for the last year."

"You never look bad. I'm just saying that you haven't gone to this much trouble in forever. What's going on?"

Keely hadn't seen her sister since before the meeting with Devon Tarlington the previous afternoon. Both Hillary and Harley had been at Brad's house, and that morning Brad alone had dropped Harley off at home. So Keely hadn't had the chance to fill her sister in.

She did it now, making sure to keep her tone neutral and her eyes on Harley as she tugged on his pajamas.

But, by the time she'd snapped the last snap and informed Hillary that Devon Tarlington would be arriving any minute to see the baby for the first time, Hillary started to laugh.

"You liked him," she accused.

"I didn't *like* like him," Keely said defensively.

"Is he beautiful?"

"He's a *guy*. Guys aren't beautiful," she said as if he were nothing remarkable, when the truth was she thought he was about the best-looking man she'd ever laid eyes on.

Hillary saw through her anyway. "Translation— he's killer-cute," her sister said.

"It doesn't matter if he is. I wouldn't touch him with a ten-foot pole."

"Why not? Does he smell bad or something?"

Keely had Harley all ready to be put down for the night as soon as Devon Tarlington accomplished what he was coming for so she picked the baby up and settled him on her hip.

"No, Devon Tarlington doesn't smell bad," she said. "But he was not happy to hear he could be a father, either. And that's the last thing I need—another guy who wants to pawn off his responsibilities on someone else."

"Oh, that reminds me!" Hillary blurted out, half-startling Harley and Keely both. "Mary called."

Keely fought to keep the pain that statement brought from showing. "When?" she asked as if it was no big deal.

'Yesterday afternoon when you went to find this Devon Tarlington person."

"I'm sorry I missed her," Keely said because it

was true, even if any contact with Mary Kent did open the wound she was still working to heal. "What did she have to say?"

As if she were reciting by rote, Hillary said, "She was just checking in to see how you are. She said she's hard to get hold of because she's almost always in class or with her friends, so don't bother calling her back. She'll try you again in a few days but she hopes the two of you can have lunch or dinner when she's home for Thanksgiving break."

"That would be nice." And not easy for Keely. But she didn't say that.

Still, Hillary knew the subject was a sore one for her sister so she changed it. "Now tell me about this Devon Tarlington guy."

"There's nothing to tell. I found him at his house and told him about Harley and Clarissa and Brian Rooney."

"How'd he take it?"

"He didn't explode or anything the way I was afraid he might. Hearing about Harley was a shock, but it didn't seem to be a big surprise that there's the possibility someone else could be Harley's father, too. He must have known Brian Rooney was in the picture—besides, something is up with that because Devon Tarlington and Brian Rooney grew up in the same small town."

"Really?" Hillary said as if that was intriguing information.

"And he doesn't like Clarissa," Keely added.

"Did you tell him to join the club?" Hillary asked

as she took one of Harley's hands and wiggled his arm enough to make him bounce.

Harley giggled and when Hillary released his hand he waved it up and down himself in an attempt to do the same thing she had.

"I didn't say anything about Clarissa except that she'd disappeared," Keely explained as if her sister's comment had been serious. "I told him she'd left us as Harley's guardians until we could figure out who the father is and hand Harley over to him."

"And Devon Tarlington wasn't thrilled with the possibility that he could be the dad?"

"No."

Hillary obliged Harley when he held his arm out for her to shake again but even as she did her brow furrowed into a frown. "Do you think even if he *is* the father he won't take Harley?"

Keely shrugged. "I don't know. He didn't say anything one way or another. Except that I think he's hoping the other guy is the dad."

"Nice," Hillary said facetiously.

"It wasn't really *not* nice. He'd just heard the news and he was shocked. Plus, obviously things with Clarissa didn't end well. It can't be a welcome possibility that he might have a child with her. Who knows? He could adjust to it and be thrilled to be a dad. After all, Harley is a pretty irresistible little dumpling," she added, nuzzling Harley's neck and making him giggle again.

"But just in case, you wouldn't touch Devon Tar-

lington with a ten-foot pole,'' Hillary reminded Keely
of her own words.

''Pretty much,'' Keely confirmed.

''Except that you got dressed up because he's coming here.''

''Maybe I just want him to eat his heart out over
what he can't have,'' Keely said with mock conceit.

''Or maybe you *like* like him and you just don't
want to admit it.''

''Even if I admit it I'm not doing anything about
it.''

''Anything but letting your hair down.''

''That's nothing. Do you really think I would be
dumb enough *ever* to get myself into another Alby
Kent situation?''

Hillary's teasing edge softened. ''I hope not. I
know I don't ever want to see you hurt like that
again.''

''Well, you don't have to worry,'' Keely assured
her.

The doorbell rang just then and Keely hated the
fact that despite all her claims, the knowledge that
Devon Tarlington was on their front porch sent a little
wave of excitement through her.

''There he is,'' she said, regretting that it came out
sounding breathless.

Hillary pushed off the doorjamb.

''I'll get it,'' she said, leaving Keely and Harley
behind in what Keely knew was her eagerness to get
a look at Devon Tarlington.

Carrying Harley, Keely followed, reaching the entry as her sister opened the door.

And when she did, there stood the man who had not been off Keely's mind since the afternoon before, looking even better than she remembered in a navy-blue Henley shirt, a sport coat and a pair of jeans.

"Hi," he said to Hillary, "I'm Devon Tarlington. And I'll bet you're Keely Gilhooley's sister."

"Hillary," Hillary countered as she opened the screen door to let him in.

He stepped inside, catching sight of Keely only then. But the moment he did, he smiled a smile that rippled from his oh-so-supple mouth all the way up to his eyes where it settled and radiated a warmth Keely thought she could almost feel.

"Hello again," she said simply enough, trying not to be affected by that megawatt smile.

"Hi," he repeated.

Then his gaze went from her to Harley and she watched tension tighten his features. "Let me guess, this must be the man in question."

"This is Harley," Keely offered, catching sight of Hillary standing behind Devon Tarlington and mouthing, *"Killer cute!"*

Hillary closed the door and joined them.

But because Keely was a little afraid her sister might say or do something to embarrass her—and maybe because she didn't want her sister intruding on this—she said, "I think we'll be okay on our own, Hill. You can get to that shower you wanted to take."

"Did I want to take a shower?" Hillary asked in mock ignorance.

"Yes, you did," Keely insisted.

Hillary let her gaze roll pointedly from Keely to Devon and back to Keely before she said, "I guess that means I'm leaving."

"Right."

"Nice to meet you," Hillary said to Devon.

"Uh, you, too," he responded, sounding confused by what was passing between the sisters.

Hillary retraced her path to the stairs but not without pausing to whisper to Keely, "This has to be who Clarissa left the other guy for."

Keely didn't respond, but instead kept her attention on Devon Tarlington and said, "Shall we do this in the living room where we can all be comfortable?"

"Whatever you think," he agreed.

Keely's and Hillary's house was similar to Devon's, only the living room was to the left of the entry. Unlike Devon's bare-necessities decorating, their home was done in a cozy French-country style, keeping to dark blues and brick reds with a dash of mustard yellow here and there to brighten it up.

The furniture was all well-cushioned and comfy. A braided rug occupied the center of the hardwood floor and a large sofa and two chairs stood around a rustic coffee table. Also unlike Devon's living room, the focal point was the antique fireplace, not the entertainment center which, in this case, was an armoire hiding a television and stereo system.

"Would you like to see if Harley will come to

you?'' Keely asked as she turned on the wrought-iron pole lamps that were sentries on either side of the couch.

''I don't think that would be a good idea,'' Devon said without a moment's hesitation. ''I wouldn't even know what to do with him. I was around babies a couple of times as a kid but my older brother did the handling. I was the go-for—you know, go for the diapers, go for the bottles, that kind of thing.''

''Your *brother* baby-sat?'' Keely said, surprised.

''It's a long story.''

And he didn't seem inclined to tell it.

Or maybe he just couldn't because he was so distracted by Harley. He was staring at the baby as if Harley were something to be wary of, something he didn't want to get too close to but had better keep an eye on.

''Why don't we sit down?'' Keely suggested, hoping to ease some of his tension.

She sat at one end of the couch, and once she did, Devon took the easy chair that gave him the most distance from her and Harley.

''I don't really know what I'm supposed to do here,'' he confessed then. ''Should I talk to him or throw him a ball or something?''

Keely had settled Harley on her lap with his back against her and she craned forward to peer down over his head to see what the infant's response was to Devon.

Harley was watching him as warily as Devon was eyeing the baby.

"He's a little young to throw a ball," Keely informed. "If one appeals to him it's usually only because he's decided to try to get it into his mouth."

"Does he always chew socks, too?" Devon asked with obvious distaste as he watched Harley gnaw at the clothing.

"It's clean," Keely assured with a laugh. "He has two teeth on bottom and he's getting more, so it must feel good on his gums. We keep it in the fridge because he also likes it cold."

"You keep socks in your refrigerator?"

"Not before Harley adopted them as chew toys. But it makes him happy."

"Can he *do* anything? Like walk or talk?" Devon asked, obviously attempting to figure Harley out.

"He crawls a little," Keely said, content to fill Devon in. "And if he's near the coffee table he'll pull himself up onto his knees. But he's pretty wobbly. And as for talking, sometimes it seems like he's trying to repeat something we've said but so far it isn't coming out as anything we can understand."

"So he's kind of like having a miniature space alien around."

Keely laughed again. Not only at what Devon said, but also at the way he said it and the forlorn expression that had his brows at odd angles above his denim-blue eyes. The whole concept of Harley really did seem foreign to him.

But still she defended Harley. "He's not an alien. He's a sweetheart."

Devon didn't appear to be convinced. But he didn't

refute her statement, either. Instead he continued his fact-finding mission. "Does he eat food or drink a bottle or—"

"Both. He eats baby food and he takes a bottle."

"Can he feed himself?"

"He can hold his own bottle. We don't give him bottles that way except at night, though. We hold him to give him his bottles through the day and then when we put him to bed at night we let him have it on his own in the crib. But we have to go in and check on him after a few minutes because he'll usually have dropped it once he's fallen asleep and we take it away then."

"Sounds like a lot of work."

And what she'd told him wasn't even a drop in the bucket.

But Keely didn't say that because she didn't want Devon any more leery than he already was. She also didn't want to mislead him, so she said, "Babies are a lot of work. But they're worth it."

"I'll reserve judgment on that," he said more to himself than to her. Then, definitely to her, he said, "Could you get him to take the sock away so I could have a look at his whole face?"

Once more, Keely bent over Harley. "I don't know. What do you say, Harley? Can the nice man see you? Can you show him your teeth?"

She tugged at the dangling end of the sock and the baby let it be pulled out of his mouth, but he didn't release his grip on it. And he ignored the request to reveal his two bottom teeth. He just continued to stare suspiciously at Devon while Devon took inventory of Harley's chubby cheeks and button nose, of his big brown eyes and the light tufts of downy, honey-colored hair.

"Can you make him smile?" Devon requested after a few moments of studying the baby.

The way he said it made Keely think he was looking for something other than Harley's two teeth. But she had no idea what and since he wasn't forthcoming she didn't feel she should ask.

"I don't know," she told him honestly. "It's his bedtime and he's not usually too jovial when he's tired."

Then, from above Harley again, she said to the baby, "Do you want to do patty-cake?"

Harley rejected the idea by putting the sock back in his mouth.

"Sorry," Keely apologized to Devon. "In the daytime he smiles a lot."

"When he does, does he have any dimples? Especially one over the corner of his mouth?" Devon asked then.

So that was what he was looking for. "No, he doesn't."

"Because my mother and my oldest brother's daughter have a dimple."

"Ah, so you wondered if Harley had one as a sign that he might be yours. No, no dimple. Actually, he resembles Clarissa pretty strongly."

"I noticed that."

Harley let his head fall heavily against Keely then,

and she knew he was fading. "I should probably get him to bed," she informed Devon without much enthusiasm. It wasn't that she wanted Harley to stay up, but she thought that since Devon had come specifically to see the infant, once Harley was gone, Devon would leave, too. Which, of course, was as it should be.

But he'd just gotten there and, even though she knew she should resist it, she didn't want him to go yet.

Then, as if her wish for more time with him had been granted, he said, "I'm curious about a couple of things. Would it be all right if we talk after he's in bed?"

"Sure," Keely agreed too quickly to leave him any doubts that she was willing.

She stood with Harley and tried to get him to wave bye-bye. But he still wouldn't let go of the sock and after a few attempts she admitted defeat. Then she took the baby to the kitchen to microwave his bottle and went upstairs to put him down for the night.

By the time she returned to the living room, Devon Tarlington had removed his jacket and, although he was sitting right where he'd been before, he seemed considerably more relaxed.

"Can I get you something to drink?" Keely offered. "Wine? Beer? Coffee?"

"No, thanks. Just your company will be great."

Okay, there was no good reason that comment should please her so much, she told herself as she sat at the end of the sofa nearest to him, curling her legs underneath her.

"Well, what do you think?" she asked bluntly then. "Besides not having the family dimple, did you see a resemblance in Harley?"

"No, I didn't. But I don't suppose that means anything one way or another."

"Probably not," Keely agreed.

"How did you and your sister get into this?" he asked then.

"By buying this house."

Devon glanced around. "How did buying this house get you involved in my potential mess? Did Harley come with it or what?"

"No, Harley didn't come with it. We just bought it and the payments are nothing to sneeze at. Neither is the upkeep. So we decided to offset some of the expense by getting a housemate and we ran an ad in the newspaper."

"And Clarissa answered it," Devon finished for her.

"She and Harley. We weren't crazy about that at first. There was only one room other than mine and Hillary's, but Clarissa insisted it didn't matter, that she and Harley could share it. After about half an hour with Harley we'd fallen in love with him, so we agreed to accept them as housemates."

"Maybe he *is* mine," Devon joked as if Harley's charm could be attributed to him.

It made Keely laugh. "I don't know, if you can't

see the benefits in chewing cold socks I have my doubts.''

"Okay then, I guess we can skip the blood test and I can just go on about my business.''

"Sorry, you're not off the hook that easily.''

Keely liked the way his face lit up when he laughed. The way tiny lines fanned out from the corners of his eyes. She liked the sound of his laughter and the fact that he had a sense of humor. But she tried not to pay so much attention to those things and went on answering his question about how she and Hillary came to be in the position they were in with Harley.

"Anyway," she said, "that was six months ago. Shortly after Clarissa moved in she began to abuse the arrangement. She was constantly asking either Hillary or me to baby-sit, and it wasn't that we minded, it was just that once Clarissa was out she didn't tend to come back when she said she would.''

"That sounds like Clarissa," Devon muttered somewhat under his breath. "What starts out seeming fun and spontaneous ends up just being irresponsible.''

"That about sums it up. Anyway, at first she'd just be a few hours late. Then she'd call and say she was spending the night with whoever she was with, she'd be back in the morning before Harley woke up. Then she started staying away for days at a time and nothing we did or said made any difference to her. She wasn't really even apologetic.''

"That sounds like Clarissa, too.''

"Last week she disappeared completely. Apparently, at some point while Hill and I were gone she'd moved her things out of the house, because she said she was running to the store while Harley napped and then she never came back. When Harley woke up and we went in to get him we realized his things were all that was left in there. Except a manila envelope that had information about the lawyer and the documents assigning Hill and me as Harley's temporary guardians, and the letter telling us either you are Harley's dad or Brian Rooney is, that we should figure out which of you it is and turn Harley over to his father."

"So she managed to give you quite a surprise, too."

"To say the least. We contacted the lawyer and he confirmed everything. Clarissa had flown the coop."

Devon was shaking his head. "Amazing."

"I'm sure we could find her," Keely continued. "But it just seems like a waste of time. Clarissa made it clear to the attorney that she doesn't want anything to do with Harley. And to tell you the truth, it isn't as if she was good for him before this. She didn't care if he was clean or fed, if he had what he needed in any way. Hill and I actually thought that she might have just left him in his crib and taken off whether we were here or not. But if you really wanted me to—"

"Don't go looking for her on my account," Devon said before she could finish that. Then he changed the subject. "But there's one thing I have been considering since you showed up at my door yesterday. I think I should be with you when you tell Brian Rooney what's going on."

"Why is that?"

"A couple of reasons. He's kind of a hothead for one and it's hard to say how he'll take this."

"Oh, so I can spring it on you but you don't think I can spring it on him?"

"I'd just feel better if you didn't have to spring it on him by yourself. Plus, just in case he does something stupid—like refuse to give blood for the test—I'd like to be there to help persuade him. Since I have a pretty high stake in this."

For a moment Keely studied Devon, wondering what form his *persuasion* might take and if it was wise to have him along when she told the other man about Harley.

He *did* have a high stake in this, she conceded. And she wasn't thrilled with the idea of being on her own when she told yet another complete stranger—a complete stranger who apparently had a short fuse—that he might be the father of Clarissa's child.

"What did you have in mind in the way of 'persuading' him if he refuses to give blood?" she asked.

Devon smiled again. "I won't bring along a baseball bat, if that's what you're afraid of. I just want to be there as your backup."

Was there a hint of flirting in that last part?

Keely couldn't be sure. But even so, it caused goose bumps to erupt up and down her arms.

"Let me think about it," she hedged, suddenly more concerned with her involuntary response to this man than with what might happen between him and Brian Rooney if she got them together.

"Okay," Devon said, easily accepting that it was her decision.

He stood then. "I should probably get going."

Keely fought a huge rise of disappointment, but she stood, too, absolutely forbidding herself to say anything to delay his departure. This was business, after all, not a social call, and their business, for the moment, was concluded.

"Have you taken Harley into the lab for his blood test yet?" Devon asked on the way to the front door once he'd replaced his sport coat.

"Not yet, no."

"Then how about if I pick you both up tomorrow and we go together?"

That caught Keely off guard.

"Harley's naps kind of dictate things," she said as they reached the entry, realizing that really wasn't an answer.

"I'm flexible. What's good for you?"

"It's usually hard to get much done until two-thirty or three in the afternoon."

"That's fine. And then after we hit the lab, how would you feel about a trip to the zoo?"

"The zoo?" Keely repeated, even more confused. Was he just trying to arrange some time to get better acquainted with Harley? Or was there something else to this?

"I've signed on to take pictures for a new fund-raising brochure—" He cut himself short and explained, "I'm a wildlife photographer. Anyway, I wanted to take a look around, get some preliminary ideas of what I might want to shoot. And since it's the zoo, I was thinking—zoo, kids—maybe you and Harley might like to go."

It seemed reasonable enough when he said it like that. And not as if he had any ulterior motives. Maybe it was just a friendly invitation to something he had to do whether they went along or not, and there honestly wasn't anything else to it. Except maybe getting more comfortable with Harley.

"Harley would love it," she admitted, making sure Devon knew the baby was the only reason she would consider it. "And I suppose it would be a good treat after putting him through whatever the lab has to do to him. It would also give the two of you more exposure to each other in case you do turn out to be father and son."

And maybe she was just rationalizing because she wanted to go. Although it wasn't the animals in the zoo that were inspiring her. It was the company she'd be keeping. She just didn't want to admit that, even to herself.

"Great," Devon said into her wandering thoughts. "Then I'll come by around two-thirty and we'll go whenever Harley wakes up."

"All right."

Devon opened the door to leave but before he did he paused.

"There's something else that keeps bothering me about this whole thing," he said then, sounding reluctant to bring it up. "You may not know the answer to this, but Clarissa never wanted to have kids. I'm surprised she went through with it."

"I do know the answer to that because she told us. But I'm not sure you want to hear it."

"I'd rather hear it than go on wondering."

"Until the letter, the only thing she said about Harley's dad was that things hadn't worked out with him and she'd gone on to greener pastures. Those 'greener pastures' involved a very wealthy man who owned a yacht and she'd taken off with him to sail the south seas."

"No sense letting any grass grow under her feet just because she'd been juggling two other men," Devon said.

"She spent several months sailing," Keely continued, "and she said she lost track of a lot of time. And since her...cycles...were never regular anyway and she'd always practiced safe sex, it didn't even cross her mind that she could be pregnant. It wasn't until after she'd started to show that she even went to a doctor and by then it was too late to terminate the pregnancy. She was pretty open about the fact that she regretted not having had that option because she would have taken it."

Actually, what Clarissa had said was that condom failure and not being able to have an abortion were the worst things that had ever happened to her, but Keely didn't want to repeat it that way.

Devon nodded. "I guess that explains it." Then he focused those blue eyes on her and smiled again. "I think Harley was lucky he fell into your hands when he did.''

Keely didn't know how to respond to that, so all she said was, ''He has us wrapped around his little finger.''

''Now I know he's *really* a lucky man,'' Devon said with a devilish grin.

He was looking at her very intently and for no reason Keely could imagine, she was suddenly struck with an overwhelming curiosity about what it might be like to have him kiss her.

Which, of course, was too ridiculous an idea to entertain, and she told herself so.

But there it was anyway—that handsome-in-the-extreme face not too far away, and those piercing eyes, and those smooth lips. And kissing was definitely what she was thinking about....

''I guess I'll see you tomorrow then,'' she blurted out, not intending to sound as if she were encouraging him to leave, but sounding that way just the same because she was in too much of a panic to escape those other, horribly inappropriate and unwanted thoughts. And inclinations.

''I'll be here,'' he assured, taking his cue and stepping out onto her porch. ''Enjoy what's left of your evening,'' he added as he headed down the steps to his waiting SUV.

Why did I have to do that? she asked herself disgustedly, wishing she hadn't just nearly kicked him out.

But even as she chastised herself she still stood

there in the open doorway and watched him go, taking in the sight of a rear end that surely qualified for derriere of the decade.

And all the while she wondered what Clarissa Coburn had gotten her into.

On a more personal level.

Chapter Three

A trip to the Denver Zoo on a sixty-eight-degree autumn afternoon when the sky was a crystal-clear blue dome and only the slightest breeze rustled through gilded leaves so bright they looked like mirror reflections of the sun? Of course Keely was looking forward to it.

And if the outing had been uppermost in her mind every minute since she'd opened her eyes that morning? And if, at two o'clock that afternoon, it was still uppermost in her mind as she headed upstairs for her bedroom to change out of her sweatsuit and primp as if she were about to embark on an important date?

She tried to tell herself it didn't necessarily mean anything. It didn't necessarily mean she was nearly pulsating with eagerness to see Devon Tarlington again. It *could* mean that she was merely looking forward to going to the zoo.

Except that she knew that wasn't true, and she couldn't let it stand. Not when she was also contemplating changing into the bra that made her look two sizes bigger under the snug-fitting split-V-neck olive sweater she'd spent too much time deciding on last night and had laid out as carefully as if it were a prom dress.

So maybe she needed to quit skirting the issue and really think this over, she told herself as she closed her bedroom door behind her.

Okay. What was it about Devon Tarlington that had her awake half the night thinking about him? What was it about him that had her distracted from her work all day with uncontrollable eagerness for this afternoon? What was it about him that had her recalling every word he'd said? Every word *she'd* said? Picturing every detail and nuance of the man?

He was drop-dead gorgeous—that was the most obvious answer. He was so handsome that she was sure heads would actually turn when he walked into a crowded room. Jaws might even drop.

And it didn't help that his looks didn't seem to be something he worked at. He didn't even seem aware that his face could have been sculpted out of marble by an old master's hand. He certainly didn't give the impression that he was concerned with it. Or affected by it. Which, of course, only increased his appeal.

Plus he had a pretty great personality. He had just enough of a bad-boy air to give him an edge. He was smart and apparently talented if he could make a living as a wildlife photographer. He was a tease, but not in a snide, hurtful way. His teasing was purely flattering.

He was also easy to talk to, and he was taking an awkward situation and doing his best to deal with it—that was no small thing even if his efforts were somewhat stilted.

And that body! Holy cow, what a body! No woman could get a glimpse of all those muscles, of all those perfect proportions, and not notice, not think about what she'd been in close proximity to, not itch to run her hands over bulging biceps and broad shoulders and hard pectorals and honed back and taut rear end.

He was just plain sexy. He exuded it in everything he did. Every movement of his hands—big, long-fingered hands. Every nod of his head. Every smile. Every everything.

All in all, what *wasn't* there to like about him? Keely asked herself as she peeled off the sweats, suddenly not only wanting to change her clothes, but needing to cool down, too.

But if she was honest with herself, there *was* one thing not to like. Well, not to *dislike* necessarily. But certainly there was one thing wrong with any scenario that revolved around him—he wasn't thrilled with the idea of being a dad. And now he might be a dad whether he liked it or not and, to Keely at least, that spelled trouble with a capital T.

Not that she didn't want kids herself, because she

did. She wanted a family. She wanted a husband—another husband—and kids.

But she wanted it all the old-fashioned way this time. She wanted to meet a great guy, fall in love with him and marry him without any strings attached. And *then* she wanted to have kids. Together. Their own kids. Mutually decided upon kids that they would both want. Kids they would be equally devoted and committed to. Kids they would both love. Kids they would both nurture and raise, together.

And unless she missed her guess, that wasn't part of Devon Tarlington's game plan.

So, on the one hand, if Devon *wasn't* Harley's dad, a relationship with him was unlikely to put her any closer to her own goals.

And, on the other hand, if Devon *did* prove to be Harley's dad, then Keely believed that any woman he brought into their lives was likely to be added as much to help with Harley, to raise Harley, as because Devon actually wanted that woman. Which was a bad basis for a relationship—something she knew only too well.

So, either way, no matter how gorgeous the guy might be, no matter how personable or how sexy, she would not let herself be swept up in anything that either cost her what she wanted in her own life, or thrust her into a situation that repeated history for her.

"Then why are you putting on this bra?" she asked herself as she did, thinking that that was the best question yet.

She wanted to pretend—as she had with Hillary the

previous evening—that it was just to make Devon Tarlington eat his heart out over what he couldn't have. But she knew that excuse wasn't any more true today than it had been last night.

And what *was* the truth was that she wanted him to notice her as much as she noticed him. She wanted him to find her as attractive. As appealing.

Even though she could have kicked herself for it.

Keely suddenly deflated onto the edge of her bed and put her face in her hands.

"What *am* I doing?" she wailed.

But as she mentally read herself the riot act, something else began to creep into her thoughts.

Maybe she was wrong about him....

It was possible, wasn't it? After all, she'd just met this guy. How, on the basis of only two brief encounters, could she say he'd probably never want kids or that he'd try to rope someone else into caring for Harley if Harley was his? Just because he hadn't welcomed the news that he could be a father didn't necessarily mean that he'd thought it was never in the cards for him or that he hadn't planned to be a participating part of the parental equation if he did become a dad.

"So maybe he should be cut some slack."

Keely got up from the bed and pulled on the olive-green sweater, bypassing the whole bra issue as this new train of thought gained some steam.

Should she cut Devon Tarlington some slack? she wondered on the way to her vanity to do her makeup.

Everyone deserved the benefit of the doubt. That

was something she'd said more times than she could count to clients who had her search for someone they weren't particularly happy with. It was a caution she gave—*Ask questions, find out the whole story before you jump to any conclusions.*

But what was she doing? She was jumping to conclusions.

So she *should* cut Devon Tarlington some slack until she knew for sure whether or not he fit into either of the slots she'd already carved out for him.

And in the meantime, maybe she should also get to know him. A little, anyway.

That thought made something else occur to Keely.

Shouldn't she get to know Devon? Didn't she have a responsibility to Harley to find out what kind of man she might be turning him over to? She was his guardian. Well, one of them, anyway. And even if, legally, she was going to have to turn the baby over to whichever man proved to be his dad, it seemed like she should know that that person would do right by the baby.

"Talked yourself into that pretty neatly, didn't you?" she muttered to her reflection in the mirror as she brushed on blusher, applied mascara and lipstick, and then finger-combed her hair to let it fall into unfettered curls around her shoulders.

Okay, sure, she had to admit that she'd managed to get around her own initial instincts about Devon Tarlington to give herself permission to get to know him. But the points were valid just the same—he didn't deserve to be prejudged and she did feel a responsibility to make sure Harley wasn't handed over to someone he shouldn't be handed over to.

And if Devon fell into one of those two slots she'd been initially inclined to put him in then at least it would be enough to put a damper on the attraction she felt for him.

"And if he turns out to be Harley's dad and you think he'll be a crummy one?" she asked herself.

But the answer to that was simple. If Devon Tarlington turned out to be the baby's father and she thought he'd make a crummy dad, she would do something about it to make sure Harley ended up in the best possible home.

And that went for Brian Rooney, too. If he was Harley's dad, Keely vowed she'd check him out and wouldn't let him have Harley until she was satisfied he'd do right by the baby.

With everything settled in her mind, Keely felt a hundred percent better. About Harley's future—which she hadn't even realized until that moment had been worrying her—and about her own course with Devon Tarlington.

She just hoped, for Harley's sake, that whoever turned out to be his father would make a good one.

And if, deep down, her hopes also had a little something to do with herself if Devon *did* prove to be the dad?

She just decided it was probably better not to go there.

"All the bad parts are over now and we just get to have fun," Keely told Harley as she unstrapped him from the infant carrier in the back seat of Devon's SUV later that afternoon.

She was glad that Harley didn't seem any the worse for wear by then and that he'd finally stopped crying. He hadn't liked the needle stick to draw blood at the lab on their last stop. His protests had been loud and Keely had felt terrible for having to submit him to anything that caused him pain.

Devon had squirmed a bit himself. Not over the procedure, but over the noise Harley had made. He was visibly embarrassed and even the nurse's assurances that she was used to it didn't seem to put him at ease.

By the end, Keely had come out of the lab unsure whether Harley or Devon had been more shaken by the experience, and between Harley's continuing lament in the car and Devon's near silence, the drive to the zoo had not been a lot of fun.

But now they were there and parked, and Harley had stopped crying and Devon seemed to have relaxed again.

"Oh, that's a nice smile," she told Harley in response to the sweet grin he gave her as she lifted him out of his car seat. Then, to Devon, she said, "See? He's fine now."

Devon looked for himself from the open hatchback of the SUV as he took out the stroller. But he still seemed wary and his only response was, "If you tell me what to do with this I'll set it up for him."

Keely gave him instructions and, by the time she

brought Harley around to the rear of the SUV, the stroller was locked in the open position and ready for the baby.

"Want to see how to buckle him into this, too?" she asked. She'd already given the demonstration on securing the car seat with seatbelts and then on strapping Harley into it, and now she showed Devon how to do the stroller as well.

"Taking him anywhere is complicated, isn't it?" he commented.

"You get used to it," she assured. "I consider it good exercise."

Devon chuckled at that. "Seems to be working," he said, giving her an appreciative smile that sent a flood of warm fuzzy feelings through Keely.

Warm fuzzy feelings she tamped down because they had no business sprouting up.

"If you'll hand me the diaper bag, it has its own place on the stroller so we don't have to carry it," she said, forcing herself back to business.

Once she had the diaper bag in place she said, "That's it. We're ready to roll."

"Just let me get my gear."

Devon closed the hatchback and went around to the side door to remove a leather camera bag from the floor behind the driver's seat, setting it on the seat to unzip it. Keely and Harley watched Devon attach a strap to the camera inside the bag and then pull it out of the case, slipping the strap over his head so it went diagonally across his broad chest. Then he loaded his

pockets with what seemed to be other lenses and giz-
mos she didn't recognize.

On a less-commanding man the camera slung
around his neck and shoulder might have looked
nerdy. It might have made him look like an over-
zealous tourist. But on Devon—dressed in jeans and
a black mock turtleneck—it only added an element of
intrigue.

With everything in place, Devon locked the car and
they headed for the zoo's entrance. He had only to
show the girl in the ticket booth a VIP card and they
were allowed free entrance.

"We'll just follow you since you're here for a reason," Keely informed Devon.

"I haven't been here since I was a kid so let's just
follow the path and look at everything," he answered.
"I need a general idea of the whole place anyway.
The pictures I take will only be preliminary, to get an
idea of angles, lighting, things like that."

Then, without warning, he raised his camera to his
eye and took a snapshot of her.

"Yuck. I hate to have my picture taken," she com-
plained, worrying instantly about her hair and if she'd
been squinting or making a funny face.

"You shouldn't hate it," he countered. "You're
very photogenic."

He said that off-the-cuff and yet still it managed to
have a flirting quality to it that brought back the warm
fuzzies for a moment before Keely got them under
control again.

They set off on the paved path that took them past the outside exhibits and to the enclosed ones.

Harley had definitely recovered from the lab trauma and since he was well-rested, he held on to the front bar of the stroller with two pudgy little hands to pull himself up straight so he could see everything.

He was particularly animated when they took him into the monkey house where there was a new exhibit of mandrills. The ferocious-looking baboons with the bright-blue-and-scarlet marked faces thrilled him, as did the African dancers that performed for the kickoff of the addition to the collection.

"Can you take him out of the stroller?" Devon asked then. "I'd like the two of you in a shot. It'll tell me if I want people in the pictures or only the animals."

"I didn't know I was signing on for surrogate model today," Keely said.

Devon grinned at her as if she'd found him out. "There'll be dinner in it for you as payment," he said with a wiggle of his eyebrows that made dinner sound like something deliciously wicked.

Keely couldn't help laughing. Or obliging him.

And that was how the remainder of the day and early evening went. They meandered through the zoo, and Harley liked just about every animal he saw. Devon made the entire excursion even more enjoyable for Keely with his teasing and flirting and irresistible charm as he took pictures of the exhibits and of Keely and Harley, too.

Afterward, good to his word, he insisted on buying

them all dinner at a kid-friendly restaurant where Harley was put into a high chair at the end of their booth.

Devon was curious about the baby's eating habits, but when Keely asked if he'd like to try feeding Harley himself, he shied away.

It was nearly nine o'clock by the time they returned to Keely's house. Devon parked at the curb, turned off the SUV's engine and faced Keely. "Would it be all right if I came in and watched you put him to bed? Just in case I end up ever needing to do that?"

After all day and evening of maintaining his distance from the baby, Keely was surprised by the request. She didn't have to give the idea much consideration, though. The alternative was saying goodnight to him right then and there. And despite the fact that she knew that was probably for the best, it didn't thrill her.

"Sure," she agreed. "You can even *do* the bedtime routine, if you want."

"I think I'll stick with being the observer for now."

"More just watching, huh?" she said, goading him slightly.

He smiled a one-sided smile. "But the view is so nice," he said, not even pretending he was talking about Harley.

This secretly pleased Keely, who hid it by saying an efficient, "Well, come on, then, it's already late for him."

Harley always enjoyed his bath and tonight was no exception. He had several tub toys Keely put in with him and he liked to slap at them to make them bob in the water.

Devon seemed to get a kick out of that from where he sat on the end of the claw-footed tub, but it still didn't inspire him to participate.

He also rejected Keely's offer to let him dry Harley off and dress him afterwards, but as she put Harley into his crib with his bottle Devon did reach a long, thick finger down to the baby, letting Harley latch on to it as Devon said a quiet and sweet, "Sleep tight, big guy."

Getting the baby to bed for the night had taken about an hour but not even the additional time had helped Keely reach the point where she was ready to see Devon go. So, as they left Harley's room, she said, "I make a mean cup of hot chocolate that tastes pretty good on these chilly fall nights. If you're interested."

"Hot chocolate, huh?" he said as if that amused him. "Clean-cut, all-American hot chocolate."

"There's wine or beer or coffee if you'd rather," she offered, confused.

But he said, "No, hot chocolate sounds good."

He followed her down the stairs as she led the way into the kitchen at the rear of the house. She hoped the bright white room that she and Hillary had decorated with touches of apple red and navy blue would keep any sense of intimacy to a minimum. A simple, friendly cup of hot chocolate at the pedestaled kitchen table—that's all this was and that's all she was determined he would think it was.

"Your sister's not around tonight?" Devon asked as she heated milk in the microwave and took two mugs from the rack under the oak cupboards.

"She's with her fiancé, helping him pack to move in with us."

"He's taking Clarissa's place?"

"Sort of. I mean, he'll be the third contributor to the house payment, but mainly he's moving in because he and Hill are getting married in less than two weeks."

"One of my brothers is getting married, too. This Saturday."

But it wasn't his family Keely was thinking about. She was stuck on his question about her sister. "Were you…interested…in Hillary?" she heard herself ask before she'd judged the question, hating that she couldn't help wondering if the whole coming-in-to-watch-Harley's-bath tonight might have been so he could meet up with Hillary again.

"I was just curious about whether we were alone or not," Devon assured her without having to think about it, leaving Keely's concerns allayed and her mind chastising her for even that moment of jealousy.

She had their mugs of hot chocolate ready by then and brought them to the table where she set one in front of Devon and took her own with her to the cane-backed chair nearest to him. She reminded herself that this was only a friendly ending to the day and nothing more, but even so—and even staying in the kitchen—there was something cozy about it all. Not to mention that sitting there alone with him was awfully nice.

"So how did you become a wildlife photographer?" she asked after their initial sips of cocoa.

"I just fell into it, to tell you the truth," he answered. "Taking one art class was a requirement in high school and at the time I thought art was only for sissies. I figured photography was slightly more macho than drawing or painting or making jewelry."

It seemed as if every fiber of her being was aware of him as a man and since she was wrestling with the potent effects of his pure masculinity it almost made Keely laugh to think of him ever having worried about appearing to be a sissy.

"And you discovered you liked to take pictures of animals?" she asked to urge him on.

"Not animals at first. I discovered I liked the view of the world through a camera lens and ended up the school photographer. When I wasn't playing football or baseball or running track I was taking the action shots for the yearbook and the newspaper—"

"Which, I assume, also meant you got to witness things like cheerleader practice," Keely guessed.

He grinned like a mischievous boy caught with his hand in the cookie jar. "Oh, yeah," he confirmed with enough lascivious emphasis to let her know that had most definitely been an ulterior motive.

Then he continued to answer her initial question about how he'd become a wildlife photographer. "I kept at it through college, studied it as an art more seriously and by the time I was ready to graduate I'd realized it might be a way to see the world. So I pounded the pavement with my portfolio until I managed to get myself hired on as the assistant to a staff photographer at a small magazine. I worked my way up to staff photographer myself, moved on to a bigger magazine, and on an assignment to Africa that I'd had to do some fast talking to get, I discovered that I had a particular knack for taking wildlife pictures. I narrowed my focus—not literally, but figuratively—risked the regular paycheck to freelance, and here I am.''

Here he was all right, Keely thought, wishing she weren't enjoying looking at that handsome face quite as much as she was.

''What about you?'' he asked then. ''How did you become a people finder, of all things?''

''I know. It's kind of weird,'' Keely said, liking that he was showing an interest in her rather than merely talking about himself. ''Hillary started out as a cop—''

''Your sister is the other part of that *we* you referred to when you told me about your business?''

So he'd been listening closely enough to recall details. She appreciated that, too.

''Right,'' she confirmed. ''Anyway, Hillary was a cop and I went from college into designing computer software. But Hill got sick of the politics and I got bored and burned out right about the time some family stuff came up. We both wanted out of what we were doing and needed to stay at home. So we hit on the idea of Where Are They Now? I had the computer know-how, Hill knew the ins and outs of investigation, and we could do it wherever we chose.''

"And you've done pretty well?" Devon asked.

"Well enough to keep at it."

Keely had barely touched her hot chocolate because she'd been too engrossed in Devon. But his was gone.

"Want another cup?" she asked with a nod toward his mug.

"It was great but I should probably get going," he said, standing and taking his cup to the sink.

Keely thought she might have heard a hint of reluctance in his voice but she couldn't be sure. She'd also run out of excuses to keep him there any longer. So, without saying anything, she took her mug to the sink, too, and then led the way to the front door.

But once they were there—and even with Devon's hand on the knob—he didn't open the door to go. Instead he turned to Keely and said, "I noticed that Harley's pajamas are kind of small for him."

She laughed lightly. "That came out of the blue," she said, because it had. "But yes, they are."

"And the sheets on his bed are threadbare and his clothes today looked pretty worn."

"Clarissa said it was a waste of money to buy too many things for someone who didn't know the difference. When she did buy him anything it was only at thrift stores or flea markets or garage sales, so it was already used and since he doesn't have much of anything, everything gets washed over and over. It makes for a lot of wear and tear," Keely explained.

"What would you say to doing some shopping for him tomorrow afternoon?"

The man really could surprise her.

"I'd say, are you sure you want to do that? Maybe you should wait until you know if he's yours or not."

"It doesn't matter. I can afford it, and even if he's not mine, I hate seeing him in too-tight, faded clothes and sleeping on rotten sheets. Just make a list of whatever he needs and let's get it for him."

"It's up to you. If you're sure," Keely said.

"I'm sure. No matter who he belongs to, kids should have what they need. I had people who made sure I did and I want to make sure Harley does."

That statement made Keely curious but she didn't think she could explore it at that moment. So she merely said, "That's really generous of you. And it would be good for him."

"It's no big deal," Devon said as if her praise made him uncomfortable.

"We could go about the same time we went to the zoo today," Keely suggested then, to get quickly past his embarrassment. "If that works for you, it works for me."

"I'll develop today's film tomorrow morning and shopping in the afternoon works out fine for me. I'll pick you up."

"Okay." And no amount of telling herself not to be so happy about that changed the fact that she was. "Thanks for the zoo and dinner tonight," she added, hoping to keep her own elation to herself.

"Thanks for the hot chocolate," he countered.

Keely laughed. "Oh, yeah, travel the world, take pictures of wild animals, be the darling of the photography world and I'm sure my hot chocolate was the high point of your life,'' she joked.

But when she glanced up at him again he wasn't laughing with her. He was smiling as if the hot chocolate really had been something he'd enjoyed.

Or maybe her company had been, because he was also staring at her with a warmth in his deep-blue eyes that she didn't think had anything to do with hot chocolate.

And suddenly she was thinking about him kissing her the way she'd imagined it at the end of the previous evening. Except that the night before she'd assumed she was the only one entertaining the idea, and tonight she wasn't so sure. In fact, she had the impression that Devon might just be thinking the same thing.

Especially since he seemed to be leaning slightly in her direction as his gaze continued to caress her face....

But then, suddenly, he drew back.

''Ooo, better not,'' he said under his breath and Keely wasn't sure she was even meant to hear it. Although, even if she had been, she could hardly say, no, it's okay, the way she was inclined to.

He finally opened her front door, letting in a gust of autumn air to chase away the heat that had seemed to radiate between them.

''Tomorrow afternoon,'' he repeated as he stepped outside, his voice deeper, more gravelly.

''We'll be here,'' she assured breezily, trying hard to ignore the fact that he had almost kissed her.

But inside she was shrieking with frustration as they said good-night and Devon left.

And no amount of telling herself it was good that he hadn't kissed her changed the fact that she absolutely would not have hated it if he had.

Chapter Four

"So...uh...I have something to tell you guys."

Devon had a full house Thursday. His brother Aiden, Aiden's fiancée, Emmy Harris, and their adopted son, Mickey, had flown in from Alaska because on Saturday they were getting married in the small town where the Tarlingtons had grown up. The eldest of the brothers, Ethan, had come in from that small town of Dunbar, Colorado, with his wife, Paris, and their baby girl, Hannah, to help with some last-minute wedding details, and everyone was staying with Devon.

At that moment Paris and Emmy and the babies were gone, and only the three men were in Devon's kitchen. They were making sandwiches for lunch when Devon said he had news.

"You aren't going to believe it," he warned. "*I* can't believe it."

"If you tell us Clarissa is back and you've forgiven her we'll have to tie you up in the basement until you come to your senses," Ethan joked.

"It's not *that* bad," Devon said. "But it does have to do with her."

"She disappeared off the face of the earth and you're being investigated for it." It was Aiden's turn to make the joke. "But if that's the case, don't worry about it. No one would be more justified in sending someone to the moon than you."

"She's disappeared, all right," Devon confirmed. "But I didn't have anything to do with it and no one is looking for her. She did, however, leave behind a little something."

"A mountain of debts in your name?" This from Ethan. "Any amount of money is worth being rid of her."

"It isn't debts," Devon said. "Although, knowing Clarissa, she probably left those behind, too, just not in my name because I was only dumb enough to let her get hold of my credit card once."

The sandwiches were made and they took their plates to the poker table Devon used as a kitchen table.

"Okay," Aiden said as they settled in to eat. "Clarissa isn't back, you haven't forgiven her— which would be insane on your part if you did— you're not under investigation for her disappearance or on the hook for her bills, but she did leave behind a 'little something.' Why don't you tell us what it is?''

''It's something that might be a sign that the universe is conspiring to tie down all the Tarlington boys at once,'' Devon said, still finding it difficult to get to the point.

''You've met a woman—Clarissa's sister or cousin or something,'' Ethan said as if to help him along.

''Oh, I met a woman all right. But she's not related to Clarissa. She's the woman who came looking for me to tell me I could be the father of Clarissa's son.''

Both Ethan and Aiden stopped eating to stare at him.

''You could be the dad?'' Aiden asked.

''*You* could be the dad?'' Ethan repeated, altering the emphasis.

''Apparently I could be.''

His brothers were obviously stunned, and silence reigned for a moment as the notion sank in.

Then Ethan said, ''You or—''

''Brian,'' Devon finished for him as if it should have been a foregone conclusion.

The introduction of that name brought about another pause in the conversation before Aiden joked, ''Wasn't it you who gave me the refresher course in safe sex when I thought Mickey might be mine?''

Mickey had been left on Aiden's doorstep and Aiden had had to consider the possibility that the baby was his until he'd discovered who Mickey really belonged to. Devon had done some good-natured teasing at the time. But these circumstances were somewhat more solemn since both Ethan and Aiden knew how difficult the situation with Clarissa had been for their brother.

Then Ethan said, "Do you have any idea which of you is most likely to be the father?"

"Not even Clarissa had an inkling and she'd have a better idea than I would, wouldn't she?"

There was no answer to that, either.

Instead Ethan said, "You could actually have a kid," obviously having trouble grasping the idea.

"His name is Harley," Devon said then. "He's eight months old. Clarissa dumped him on two women she was sharing a house with. She left instructions to find me…and Brian…to determine paternity, and she's already legally relinquished custody to whichever of us proves to be the father."

Both his brothers were still at a loss for words and another moment passed before Aiden said, "So how do you feel about this?"

"Blown away," Devon admitted. "I mean, me? A father? How the hell could that happen?"

"Condom failure?" Ethan suggested.

"I didn't mean *literally.* I meant it's unthinkable. I'm about the last guy in the world who's prepared to be a dad. Plus, I've been to Keely's place, watching what she does with this baby, supposedly trying to get comfortable with him or used to him or get to know him or something, and it's just not happening. I just can't get into it."

His brothers laughed sympathetically.

"That'll pass," Ethan said. "You just don't have any experience with babies or kids."

Devon wasn't reassured. But since he knew that these were the two people he could always be completely honest with, he did confess. "I also don't feel paternal. I don't have any urge to hold him or to even get within fifty feet of him. I just keep thinking what if he *is* mine? What the hell am I going to do with him?"

"No one knows better than I do how much of a shock this is," Ethan said. "But I'm living proof that it can all work out for the best."

Ethan was referring to the fact that only a few months earlier he'd returned from an extended business trip out of the country to discover that he had Hannah.

"When did you find this out?" Aiden asked.

"Monday."

"So it's just been a few days. No wonder you're still reeling," Aiden said. "I know the first couple of days after I was left with Mickey everything almost seemed surreal. But look at me—I ended up wanting him enough to adopt him even though he *wasn't* mine."

"We're different, though, A. We lead different lives," Devon pointed out. "What am I going to do with a baby? Pack him in my camera case to take him along to India or Africa or the Himalayas?"

"I didn't say it would be easy," Aiden agreed. "I'm just saying that if you have a son, he might be worth the trouble and some alterations in your life-style.''

"That's what Keely said—that Harley was worth it all. But it didn't help when she said it, either,'' he finished morosely.

"Are the wheels in motion to figure out which of you is the father?'' Ethan asked, settling into problem-solving mode.

"I went in for the blood test yesterday,'' Devon answered. "But Keely hasn't found Brian yet. I knew he was leaving Denver but I don't know where he went. I told Keely to start looking for him in Dunbar, that maybe his family knows where he is. The whole thing is just a big damn mess.''

"I know this has you shaken up,'' Aiden said. "That's to be expected. But it really will all work out. If the baby is yours, things'll fall into place. You'll see.''

Devon didn't say anything to that. Aiden was a physician and his approach was what it might be if he were telling a patient that the effects of a new medication he'd prescribed would eventually subside. It didn't help Devon any more than Ethan's problem-solving angle.

"I don't know how things will fall into place if he's mine,'' Devon insisted. "The more time I spend around Harley, the more convinced I am that I'd make a lousy father. I'm telling you, I don't feel anything for this baby. Not the way you said you felt with Hannah the minute you laid eyes on her, Ethan.''

"It'll come," Ethan said confidently. "Babies have a way of getting under your skin."

"Women get under your skin. But babies? I don't know about that," Devon countered.

"Speaking of women," Aiden said, taking advantage of the opportunity to get off the other subject. "Who is this Keely you keep referring to?"

"She's one of the women Clarissa left Harley with. She and her sister have temporary custody. She's great."

Something about the way he'd said that last part alerted his brothers, because Aiden and Ethan looked as if their antennae had gone up.

"She's great, huh? As in 'great with the baby' or 'great-looking' or just 'all-around great'?" Ethan probed.

"All of the above," Devon said, actually feeling better as the image of Keely came into his mind. "She's so good with Harley you'd think he was hers. She's sweet and kind and funny and smart. And she's beautiful—she has the most gorgeous long, curly red hair you've ever seen. Big green eyes. Skin like porcelain. A compact little body..."

Devon realized belatedly that he might be saying more than he needed to about Keely and cut himself off. "Like I said, she's great," he concluded, forcing a more neutral tone than he'd used before.

But it was too late. He'd already alerted the troops.

"Are we hearing a touch of interest in your voice?" Ethan asked.

"No," Devon was quick to answer.

Maybe too quick.

"She's beautiful and smart and kind and funny and sweet. She has hair and a face and body to make you wax poetic. And you want us to believe you aren't interested?" Aiden said with a laugh.

"She's also a girl-next-door type, just like Patty," Devon answered with the full impact of that fact in his voice.

But Ethan wasn't going along with it. "There's a lot to be said for the girl-next-door type."

"For you, maybe," Devon said, referring to Paris. "But you know the whole girl-next-door thing didn't work out for me any better than the wild-woman thing did."

"But if you have a kid a lot of things will change and you might find that type has more appeal than it used to," Ethan said.

Devon shook his head. "You just think everyone should be as domesticated as you are now."

"That's because I'm happy and I want you to be happy, too. It's worked for Aiden."

"I don't think I could be much happier," Aiden chimed in.

Devon stood and took their empty plates to the sink to escape all that bliss that he thought blinded them to the realities of his life.

"Maybe you should just try rolling with this whole situation," Ethan suggested. "The baby. The woman..."

"Right. And for a living I could take graduation

pictures in the backyard and hope I don't go stir-crazy,'' Devon said sarcastically.

Sarcastically enough, apparently, for his brothers to back off from trying to convince him domestication would work out for him when they should have known as well as he did that it wasn't likely.

Instead, Aiden merely said, ''It'll all be okay, Dev. One way or another.''

''Right,'' Devon said without much conviction.

But the one thing that did feel okay—actually better than okay, the one thing that felt good—was the fact that in a couple of hours he'd get to see Keely again.

And while he knew that, given what he'd just said to his brothers, it didn't make much sense, it was still true. He couldn't wait to be with her again.

Baby or no baby.

Girl-next-door notwithstanding.

Harley woke up early from his nap that afternoon so Keely had him ready to go shopping by the time Devon arrived. In fact, she was standing with the baby at the living-room window, holding him on her hip, as Devon parked his SUV at the curb in front of her house.

''Here he comes,'' she whispered to the infant with too much excitement in her tone as she watched Devon get out of the vehicle and come up the walk with a long-legged, sexy swagger.

He was wearing jeans and a navy-blue Henley T-shirt that hugged his mile-wide shoulders and impressive chest. Merely the sight of him made Keely's mouth go dry even though she'd had a firm talking-to with herself about controlling just that kind of response to him. She was determined that she would remain impervious to all of his charms, that she would be unmoved by his appeal, that she would approach this afternoon in a businesslike manner to the end.

Yet there she was already—with a catch in her throat at nothing more than her first glimpse of him.

"I really am going to be above it all today, Harley. I really, really am," she informed the infant as if he knew what she was talking about.

But, in spite of all her best intentions, she still moved away from the window and hurried to the front door to open it before Devon had the chance to knock.

"Am I late?" he asked when she'd whipped open the door, apparently noticing her eagerness and misconstruing it.

"No, we just saw you coming," Keely answered as if she hadn't been waiting—with bated breath—for him.

She pushed open the screen and Devon stepped into the entryway, giving her a quick once-over that she didn't think she was supposed to see. But she did see it. Along with the slight smile of approval that gave a boost to her ego and made her glad she'd opted for her new low-waisted jeans with the body-hugging tan turtleneck.

"Just let me get Harley into his coat and we can go," Keely said, leading the way into the living room where she had the baby's car seat waiting and his diaper bag packed.

"I think the stroller is still in my car," Devon said as she slipped on Harley's miniature jean jacket.

"I thought it must be when I couldn't find it. I guess we didn't take it out after the zoo yesterday."

Devon chuckled slightly all of a sudden. "I can't believe I'm standing here, talking about this. It's so weird. Doesn't it strike you that way sometimes? I mean, you're an unmarried person without kids of your own, taking care of this *baby*. Every now and then don't you just stop and think, *what's going on here?*"

Keely didn't want to get into why it wasn't all that strange to her so she skipped over his questions and asked one of her own. "You're really having trouble getting used to this idea, aren't you?"

"You'll never know how much trouble I'm having," Devon said with another chuckle, this one wry.

"I can imagine how difficult it would be to find yourself potentially the parent of a ready-made child."

"*Ready-made*—that's a good way to put it. Maybe if I'd begun with the starter kit—"

"The starter kit?" Keely repeated with a laugh of her own.

"You know, like if I was in a relationship, if my partner got pregnant and we decided to have the baby, if I had nine months to prepare—maybe I'd be handling this whole thing better. Maybe a little lead-up would have helped."

"I'm sure it wouldn't have hurt. Then you would have reached parenthood by degrees. As it is—"

"As it is, I don't know which end is up," Devon finished for her.

Keely couldn't help smiling at him. "I'll bet this is the only thing in your whole life that's ever had you this unhinged."

This time Devon laughed outright. "Terrific. Now you think I've gone nuts."

"Well, not completely," she teased.

Keely belted Harley into the car seat once she had his jacket buttoned and announced, "Okay, we're all set. Think you can hold it together long enough to shop?"

"Why? Do I look like I might take off any minute and run screaming into the distance?"

"Maybe not screaming into the distance, but I have to wonder if sometimes you aren't thinking about running the other way."

That made him laugh once more, his face erupting into lines and creases that only made him more terrific-looking. "If I confess that there's a part of me that wants to do that will you think I'm pond scum?"

"I'll think you're human. Besides, it isn't what a small part of you wants to do that would make you pond scum. Actually doing it would make you pond scum."

"Well, I'm not going to. It's just that yeah, you're right, the occasional thought does skip naked through my mind."

The idea of even a naked *thought* in conjunction

with Devon was too titillating for Keely to endure and she had to work at maintaining her control.

"So, if you're not going to run screaming into the distance, shall we go?" she said, hoping to escape either his appeal or her own response to it.

Devon grabbed the car seat by its handle and left only the diaper bag for Keely.

"Okay," he said with a sigh. "Where to?"

Keely had considered the best place to find what Harley needed and, as they headed out of the house, she told him she'd decided on a retail store that catered only to infants and children.

After Keely took over the chore of strapping the carrier into the back seat, she and Devon got into the front of the SUV themselves and Devon drove them there.

He spared no expense on their shopping trip. Rather than keeping their purchases to the bare minimum he made sure Harley was well-outfitted with baby equipment, clothes, shoes, diapers and even toys.

Keely was surprised and impressed with his generosity, but even as he got into the swing of it and seemed to be enjoying himself, she also noted that he still kept himself as removed from Harley as possible. Devon just didn't relate to or interact with the infant, and by the end of the afternoon it occurred to Keely that that might be part of why he'd gone overboard in his gift-giving—he was trying hard to compensate for his hands-off attitude toward the baby.

The idea spurred memories for Keely that should have blunted her attraction to him.

The problem was, he'd also managed to be such good company that her attraction to him was flourishing anyway. And as they returned to her house at dusk all she could think was that it seemed like no time at all had passed since they'd left and now it was over.

No sooner had she found her spirits dropping, than Devon parked at the curb, turned off his engine and angled in her direction to say, "I know this is last-minute, but you wouldn't happen to be free tonight, would you?"

"Tonight? You mean, like, right now?" she said as if she weren't having to fight to keep herself from sounding thrilled by that simple inquiry.

Devon had the good grace to look ashamed of himself. "I mean like maybe in an hour or so. But if you want to tell me to blow it out my ear for not asking earlier, I'll understand."

"I guess I should hear what it is you're asking."

"My brother Aiden and his fiancée and their baby came in from Alaska late last night, and my other brother Ethan, his wife and their daughter drove in from Dunbar to meet them. They're all staying at my place and we're having dinner tonight. Nothing fancy, we're just going out for pizza—kids included. I wondered if you…and Harley…might come with me. I didn't say it before because I thought it would be sort of overwhelming to have the whole gang in your face at once, but—"

She thought he was going to say, *but on second thought, I'd like them to meet Harley.* So, thinking to beat him to the punch, she said, ''If you just want to take Harley to show him to your family, I don't need to be included.''

''I do want Aiden and Ethan to see him, to see if there's any resemblance I might have missed,'' Devon conceded. ''But the truth is, if babies weren't on the guest list tonight I'd still be asking you to come. I probably shouldn't admit this, but this afternoon has just been too damn short.''

Something suspiciously like delight skittered all through Keely at that. At that and at the warmth in his eyes when he said it.

And even though she knew she should stay the course she'd set for herself today and decline the invitation, she heard herself say, ''I don't have anything planned for tonight and dinner with your brothers sounds like fun. I'd like to meet them.'' Then, as if to make it more acceptable, she added, ''And it probably *would* be good for them to see Harley.''

Devon grinned as if she'd just granted him something he'd wanted and hadn't been sure he would get. ''Great. I need to check in with everybody to make sure where we're going, but do you think you can make it if I'm back in an hour or so?''

''Do I need to change?''

Devon didn't so much as glance downward. ''Not a thing,'' he said with a wicked edge to his voice. Then, as if he'd misunderstood the question, he said,

"Oh, you mean do you need to change clothes. No, you look pizza-perfect."

"Pizza-perfect?" she parroted with yet another laugh.

But he didn't address his wordplay. Instead, in a more intimate voice, he said, "We aren't going anywhere fancy with three kids in tow. We'll save fancy for another night. When maybe there's just the two of us."

Keely didn't say anything to that. She didn't even want to think about a night alone with him for a fancy dinner. It was just too dangerous an idea to entertain, and she was already doing something she probably shouldn't by going out with him tonight. Even if it was with his family.

"I'll change Harley into some of his new clothes," she said then, attempting to keep the goal of showing the baby to Devon's brothers as the real reason for the evening to come. "And we'll be ready when you get here."

Devon smiled a pleased smile that had a tinge of the bad boy to it. "Great."

Then he helped get Harley and all the things he'd bought the baby up to the house before reminding Keely he'd return in an hour and leaving her.

Leaving her to try to recorral her own pleasure at the thought that she only had an hour before she got to see him again.

The pizza parlor was a neighborhood restaurant that Keely knew well. Devon's brothers and their families were already seated and waiting for them when they arrived.

Devon made the introductions as Keely sat Harley in a high chair identical to the two that held Devon's adorable niece and nephew.

"So this could be our boy, huh?" Ethan said when the amenities were over and Keely had taken the chair next to Harley while Devon sat on her opposite side.

"See anything that shouts Tarlington?" Devon asked as all eyes went to the baby.

"I don't. But that doesn't mean anything," Aiden answered.

"He doesn't have Mom's dimple like Hannah does—that was my first clue with her," Ethan contributed.

"He's awfully cute, though," Ethan's wife Paris offered as if that might help if Harley turned out to be Devon's child.

"And he's a good baby, aren't you, Harley?" Keely offered in the same vein.

"But what are the odds of all three Tarlington brothers ending up with babies under unusual circumstances?" Emmy, Aiden's fiancée, asked.

"I would have thought it was impossible to happen even twice. But look at you and Aiden," Ethan said.

"What kind of unusual circumstances are we talking about?" Keely felt free to ask since the Tarlingtons had brought up the subject in the first place.

Both couples jumped at the chance to tell her the stories of how they'd ended up together and with babies.

Hannah was the result of an unprecedented night of passion between Ethan and Paris just before Ethan had left the country. But he hadn't been able to forget about Paris and had looked her up almost the moment he'd returned, only to discover he was a father.

Aiden and Emmy had met when Emmy had gone to Alaska to evaluate the small town of Boonesbury for a medical grant. The same night she'd arrived, Mickey had been left on Aiden's doorstep. After discovering that he wasn't Mickey's father, and after Emmy had given up everything to move to Alaska to be with him, they'd adopted the abandoned baby.

"And we're about to live happily ever after," Emmy concluded as she and Aiden shared a kiss.

Then Aiden said, "If you'd like to come to the wedding, Keely, we'd love to have you there. It's Saturday."

"So I've heard," Keely said.

She didn't go beyond that to answer the invitation one way or another but nobody seemed to notice as their pizzas were served, and once they'd all begun to eat, the subject changed.

As the evening progressed Keely did have fun, though. Devon's brothers were as charming as he was and watching them tease each other, witnessing the closeness they shared—the same kind of closeness Keely shared with her sister—made her feel right at home.

Good looks also ran in the family, and Keely had the opportunity to study the strong resemblance among the brothers. It was impossible to say which of them was more handsome than the others, yet, for no reason Keely could pinpoint, her attraction was solely for Devon.

Actually, she felt more than the attraction to him. She started to even feel a connection with him. As if they were as much a couple as Ethan and Paris, or Aiden and Emmy. And no amount of telling herself to curb it caused that to happen.

By the time dessert was served, both of the other babies were nestled in their fathers' laps. But again it was only Keely tending to Harley—a fact that wasn't lost on Devon's brothers because Ethan said, "I haven't seen you lay a hand on that baby, Devon. Are you afraid of him?"

The eldest Tarlington was clearly goading the youngest, but Devon thwarted the attempt by saying, "I'm terrified of him," and making everyone at the table laugh.

"Maybe you just need some lessons," Aiden suggested, not letting Devon off the hook so easily. "Pass Harley to him, Keely, and we'll tutor old Devon, here."

Keely wasn't sure what to do. She was holding Harley on her lap and that was where she left him as she shot Devon a questioning glance, knowing how steadfastly he'd avoided all contact with Harley except for occasionally letting the infant grab on to his finger.

"Go on, Keely, give Harley to him," Ethan urged before Devon had given her any sign as to what he wanted her to do.

"Okay, fine," Devon finally said, as if he were accepting a challenge to jump off a cliff. "Give him to me."

"You're sure?" Keely said quietly.

"How hard can it be if these two can do it?" he said, giving a little of what he'd been getting back to his brothers.

Keely shrugged. "Okay."

She transferred Harley from her lap to one of Devon's massive thighs.

But Devon was hardly a natural. Rather than embracing the infant or moving him to rest against him, he cupped one big hand around the baby's shoulder as if it were a basketball, maintaining distance between them even then.

"Put your arm around him, for crying out loud," Ethan said with another laugh. "Support him in the crook of your arm."

Devon did as his brother instructed but all the actions that moved Harley closer were painfully awkward and the arm he wrapped around the baby was as stiff as a board.

"Relax," Aiden said, seeing Devon's tension. "He's not a porcupine. You look like you're afraid you're going to get stuck or something. And he'd probably feel more secure if you'd put your other hand on his stomach to keep him up straight."

Devon followed that advice, too, but gingerly, making everyone laugh again.

"Geez, Dev, you're really lousy at that," Ethan observed. "I guess you should've done a little of the baby-sitting you always skipped out on when we were kids.''

Devon didn't say anything to that but Keely thought it was evident in his expression that he wasn't sorry for not participating in whatever baby-sitting his older brothers had done in their youth. He was only sorry to have Harley in his lap now.

And Harley must have sensed Devon's uneasiness because he got fussy and Keely ended up taking him back before Devon panicked.

''Man, you'd better do some practicing, just in case,'' Ethan said.

It was eight o'clock by then and all three babies were ready for the evening to come to a conclusion, so the check was paid and packing up began.

Again, as Ethan and Aiden played a part in getting their babies' coats on, Keely alone accomplished the task with Harley.

Devon did put Harley's bottle, toys and bib back in the diaper bag, so it wasn't as if he just sat there. It was only when it came to dealing directly with Harley that he had a problem.

Good-nights were said to Keely in the parking lot. Devon assured his brothers he'd be home right after dropping Keely and Harley off and then he, Keely and Harley were back in Devon's SUV, headed for Keely's house.

It seemed to Keely like the prime opportunity to satisfy some of her curiosity, so she said, ''You mentioned that Ethan did some baby-sitting when you guys were kids and he said it again tonight. I didn't know many boys who baby-sat. What was it, his first foray into being an entrepreneur?''

Devon chuckled slightly. ''No, it was just a chore he was given at a few of the homes where we stayed.''

Keely looked at Devon's profile in the illumination of the dashboard and the streetlights they passed and even her increasing curiosity didn't keep her from appreciating the sight.

''It was a chore at a few of the homes where you stayed?'' she repeated. ''What does that mean?''

He glanced over at her, probably judging whether or not to get into it all.

But then he smiled a small, sad sort of smile and said, ''Our parents were killed in a car accident outside of Dunbar when I was eight. Aiden was nine. Ethan was ten.''

''Oh. I'm sorry,'' Keely said, wondering if she shouldn't have gotten into this after all.

''It's okay. It was a long time ago. It isn't a sore subject,'' he assured her. Then he went on, ''We didn't have any aunts or uncles or grandparents, so we were orphaned. Dunbar was a small, close-knit community and they didn't want to see us put into foster care and probably split up. The trouble was, no one was making a whole lot of money. Ethan has revived the economy by bringing Tarlington Software to town, but back then, times were tough, so no single family could afford to take us in. But everybody got together and decided that wasn't going to matter. They started a fund that everyone donated to in order to support us and we went from family to family to live. A few months here, a few months there…''

"They passed you around?" Keely said, thinking that was nearly as bad as if they'd been in the system.

But Devon was quick to correct that impression. "It might have been that way literally, but that wasn't how they made us feel. We felt wanted in every home. We'd spend time with one family and then someone would come over and say, *Hey, guys, we have a new litter of puppies and we thought you three might want to come stay with us to play with them.* Or, *We're planning to do a lot of boating this summer, boys. How about you come with us?* Looking back on it, we figure it must have all been prearranged, but it was done so that we always felt welcome.''

"So it was okay?" Keely asked.

"It was a lot more okay than if we'd been shipped off to Denver to be separated into different foster homes with strangers. We were kept together—that was a big thing, having each other—and we never went without what our friends had so we never felt all that different from everyone else.''

Keely recalled something he'd said the previous evening when he'd offered to outfit Harley. "That's what you meant about kids deserving to have what they need and that you had people who made sure you did, isn't it?''

"Yep," he admitted. "When everybody else got new school clothes, we got new school clothes. If we wanted bicycles for Christmas, we got bikes for

Christmas. And I'm not talking hand-me-downs. I'm talking new stuff, just the same as the other kids.'' Devon smiled a half smile and looked at her out of the corner of his eye. ''Of course we also got reprimanded and punished the same as the other kids when we stepped out of line. And we had chores to do, and responsibilities. We were just part of all the families.''

''And that was how Ethan did the baby-sitting?''

''That's how. We took out the trash or mowed the grass. Ethan—being the oldest—had to do some baby-sitting. Plus there were rules we had to follow, curfews, manners that had to be minded. It really was just like having a whole slew of parents.''

''You must have a long Christmas card list.''

He laughed. ''Pretty long.''

They'd reached Keely's house by then. Devon parked in front and turned off the engine. ''So there you have it—the strange story of my childhood.''

''It *is* pretty strange,'' Keely agreed, teasing him. ''Maybe that explains why you're so freaked out at the possibility of being tied down now. You've never learned how to stay in one place for very long.''

''I hadn't thought of it like that, but you could be right. I know I didn't mind the moving around. In fact, I kind of liked it. Always something new and different. I never got bored.''

''I guess that was probably a good thing,'' Keely said. ''Then, anyway. It might not be such a good thing now, though,'' she added with a glance in the back seat where Harley was sound asleep.

''Mmm,'' Devon agreed a bit wryly as he got out

of the SUV, closed his door as quietly as he could, and opened the rear door to get Harley out.

Keely led the way up the walk, thinking too much about the fact that Devon had told his brothers he'd be right home. It meant that he couldn't linger the way he had the last two evenings.

She unlocked the front door and they went inside, but as soon as Devon had set the car seat and Harley on the floor near the stairs, he confirmed that he wouldn't be going beyond the entryway tonight. "I should probably just leave Harley here for you to put to bed so I can go play host back at my place."

"Sure. That's fine," Keely said, trying to hide her disappointment.

"Will you be okay getting him upstairs and everything?"

Keely laughed. "I think I can handle it."

"Aiden and Ethan and I have to pick up our tuxedos tomorrow and then there's the wedding rehearsal. Even though the wedding will be at Ethan's house in Dunbar it was easier for everyone to get to the rehearsal if we had it in Denver. And then afterward we're throwing Aiden's bachelor party, so I probably won't see you," he said, sounding as if he wasn't at all happy about that.

"I should do some work on finding Brian Rooney," Keely contributed since they seemed to be exchanging agendas for the next day.

Devon nodded, his eyes never leaving her face as they stood there at the door.

"And then Saturday is the wedding," he reminded.

It was Keely's turn to nod.

"It would be nice if you'd come. We could bring Harley, too. Ethan has a full-time nanny who'll help with him. Hannah and Mickey will be there, along with other kids, I'm sure. We could make a weekend of it. Ethan's house is huge. Harley would be in the nursery and you'd have your own bedroom and bath. I'd give you the tour of Dunbar...."

He said that as if he were offering to show her around Rome or London and Keely couldn't help smiling up at him.

"I'll have to think about it," she said, to buy herself some time. Not that she needed to think about whether or not she wanted to go. Not only did it sound like fun, but the idea of spending the weekend with Devon had more appeal than he would ever know. Which was exactly the reason she knew she shouldn't jump into anything.

"You're not a woman who makes snap decisions, are you?" he said then.

"Sometimes I am," she defended herself.

"Just not with me. You're thinking about whether I can go along with you when you tell Brian Rooney about Harley, and now you'll have to think about going to the wedding."

"In this case, snap decisions might get me into trouble," she pointed out.

"A little trouble can spice up your life," he joked with an edge of lasciviousness to his voice.

"My life is plenty spicy," she countered, but in a tone not too different from his.

He was staring down into her eyes, delving into them as though on a quest for something, for seeing into her soul, maybe. And Keely was looking into the deep-blue depths of his, too, wondering what there was about this man that had such a powerful effect on her that she kept doing—and wanting to do— things she absolutely knew weren't wise. Things like the evening that had just made her feel coupled with him. Things like agreeing to a weekend with him. Things like kissing him…

"You should probably get home to your family," she forced herself to say.

"Probably," he agreed, his voice quiet, intimate, sexy now as he moved a step closer to her. "It's just that something keeps telling me that once I walk out the door it could be quite a while before I get to see you again."

"You'll be so busy with the wedding you won't even think of me."

"Oh, I'll think of you, all right. I'm having a hell of a time thinking about much else. In fact, if you don't come to Dunbar with me, it could actually ruin the whole wedding—the whole weekend—for me," he said with an edge of mischief now.

"Really? The *whole* wedding and the *whole* weekend?"

"Everything," he confirmed. "But you could fix that just by telling me right now that you'll come. You and Harley."

She merely smiled enigmatically, still not committing to anything.

"So what do you say?" Devon coaxed. "Just take the plunge and tell me when to be here Saturday morning to pick you guys up."

"I can't do that. I have to check with my sister and see if she needs me. I might have to work. There are a lot of variables."

"It's the weekend—that means no work."

"Not necessarily."

"So you'll just think about it," he repeated in a monotone.

"I'll think about it."

"And in the meantime you'll leave me hanging in the balance? Not knowing if I'm going to have to go stag to my own brother's wedding?"

"I have confidence that you'll survive one way or another."

"You're a hard woman," he said affectionately.

"I know," she agreed, his words delighting her.

He must have been delighted, too, because he was grinning, and his eyes still held hers.

Then he leaned forward to whisper in her ear, "I guess I'll just have to call you tomorrow to get your answer."

"I guess you will," she said, trying not to let the citrusy, tangy scent of his aftershave go to her head.

He straightened up again. But not completely. Instead he was very near as he peered down at her once more.

And then he did kiss her. But only a quick one. A brief brushing of his lips against hers as if he were giving her the barest of sneak previews to tip her decision in his favor. Too quick for her to really feel it. Certainly too quick for her to return it.

Just when she hoped for a second kiss, a second chance, he took a step backward, away from her.

"I'd better go," he announced, obviously unsure what he might do if he didn't.

Keely didn't agree with him. She didn't say anything at all because she was afraid if she opened her mouth she would beg him to stay. Or, at the very least, to kiss her again.

"'Night," he said with a wicked grin, as if he knew what was going through her mind.

"Good night," Keely managed.

Then Devon slipped out her front door, leaving her to take care of the baby that might be his while he went on his way.

But not even the sharp flashback to her marriage that that caused her was enough to change what she was feeling.

And what she was feeling was that she wanted nothing so much as to see him again, regardless of what it might mean down the road.

Well, nothing so much as to see him and maybe to have him kiss her again....

Chapter Five

"Knock, knock! It's only me. Can I come in?"

"Sure," Keely called, without opening her eyes. She was lying back in a bathtub full of bubbles at a little after ten the following night.

Hillary only opened the door as much as she had to to slip inside and then closed it again after herself. "Bad day?" she asked.

"Long day," Keely amended. "And I'm rewarding myself."

Only her head and arms were outside of the bubbles. Her head was resting on a bath pillow Hillary had given her last Christmas, and her arms were braced by the tub's edges. When she heard her sister lower the hamper lid she knew Hillary hadn't just come in for an aspirin or something. She was perching there to talk. So she opened her eyes and turned her head in Hillary's direction.

"Are you finished with the move?" Keely asked.

"The closing was this morning, and, as of ten minutes ago, Brad is our new roomie," Hillary said. "You now have a man living with you."

"I bought him a welcome-to-the-household six-pack of that ale he likes. It's in the fridge," Keely informed her.

"That was nice. I'll tell him. So how's Harley?"

"Good. He's always good. I got him to bed about an hour ago."

"I'll be able to do a little more with him now that the move is over," Hillary said.

"I haven't minded. He's an easy baby," Keely assured her.

"Still, tomorrow morning you can sleep in and I'll get him up."

"Great." Keely's arms were getting chilly so she pulled them into the water. "Did you see those two packages that were delivered for you and Brad today?" she said then.

"We already opened them. They were wedding presents. One of them was the lamp from Aunt Gladys—it must be fifty years old. The shade has ducks and geese all over it and fringe around the bottom. The other one was from Mary."

Mary.

Keely mentally tried to sidestep the twinge of pain that rose at just the mention of her former step-daughter's name.

"What did she send?" she asked without letting her reaction show.

"A really beautiful crystal dish. And a note. She isn't coming for the wedding. Homecoming is the same weekend, and she's been nominated for queen."

An odd combination of feelings washed through Keely. Relief. Disappointment. Regret. Pride.

But again she kept her feelings to herself and instead addressed only the homecoming-queen portion of what her sister had just said.

"Straight As and homecoming queen, too? She's come a long way from that painfully shy little girl she used to be, hasn't she?"

"She blossomed by the time she got to high school," Hillary reminded. "And all because of you."

"It wasn't me who tried out for cheerleader when she was in high school—and made it—and I'm not going to her classes or wowing people enough to make them want her for homecoming queen now. Those are her accomplishments, not mine," Keely demurred.

"But you're who got her there in the first place. You're who built up her self-esteem and gave her the confidence and the support. Without you—"

"Did she have anything else to say?" Keely asked, cutting into her sister's stream of thought rather than let it continue.

Hillary paused as if she might go on anyway. But then she conceded and said, "She wanted me to tell you she's sorry she hasn't had time to call you again after missing you the last time, but she's been swamped. She still wants to see you sometime over the holidays when she's home from school. She said to give you her love, and she sent you three pictures of her apartment—she's obviously excited to be out of the dorm for the first time because in one of the photographs she's jumping up in the air.''

That sounded like the exuberant girl Keely still missed so much it hurt.

"I brought the pictures in with me," Hillary said then. "Want to see them now or should I leave them for you to look at when your hands aren't wet?''

"Leave them," Keely said, hating that her voice cracked when she spoke.

If her sister heard it she didn't say anything. She just reached over and set the prints on top of the tissue box on the toilet tank.

The sound of Keely's soon-to-be brother-in-law calling Hillary's name came from just outside the bathroom door then.

"Go down to the kitchen. I'll be right there," Hillary called back. Then to Keely she said, "Brad's starving and I promised to fix him something to eat since he doesn't know where anything is yet. So I better go do it.'' She got off the hamper. "What about you? Are you going to bed after your bath or should I make you a sandwich, too?''

Keely had actually been planning on having a snack but she'd suddenly lost her appetite. "Thanks, but I'm not hungry. I think I'll just go to bed.''

"Okay. Remember, I'll take care of Harley in the a.m. so you can sleep late if you want."

"The perfect Saturday morning," Keely said by way of confirmation as her sister left the bathroom as carefully as she'd entered it.

Keely straightened her head on the pillow and closed her eyes.

But the water was beginning to cool and she didn't feel all that relaxed anymore, so she opted for ending her soak.

She pulled the plug on the drain and stepped out onto the bath mat, grabbing a big fluffy towel to dry off. But as she did her eyes went to those photographs her sister had left. She knew that was the cause of the tension that was back in her neck and shoulders and she had to wonder at fate's timing of Mary's gift and note and pictures.

Keely had just spent the day thinking about whether or not to go to Dunbar with Devon for his brother's wedding, and just when she was leaning toward indulging herself by going, here was this reminder of exactly the reason she should be keeping her distance from Devon. Here was the reminder of the lesson she'd learned the hard way.

Maybe it was a sign, she thought. A sign that she shouldn't go.

She knew she'd already done more with Devon than she should have, and maybe this was just the wake-up call she needed to keep her from doing anything more. Maybe it was the warning that she should keep as much distance from Devon as possible, that she should make absolutely sure that their relationship didn't go any further than it had. It should be strictly business from here on, business that required only that she inform him when she found out whether or not he was Harley's father. She could do that over the telephone, and if he *was* Harley's father, she only had to meet with him once to hand Harley over.

Clean. Quick. Uninvolved. Safe.

No more trips to the zoo. No more dinners with his family. No more late-evening talks after Harley was asleep. No letting him go with her to tell Brian Rooney about Harley. And absolutely no weekends away with him. And in order to be sure whoever ended up with Harley was a fit parent, she would merely make a call to Social Services and have them evaluate the situation.

Keely slipped into her flannel pajamas, gathered her dirty clothes and damp towel to drop into the hamper, and turned to leave the bathroom.

But she couldn't do that without taking those pictures from Mary with her.

And she knew if she picked them up, she would have to look at them.

So get it over with, she told herself.

She snatched them from the top of the tissue box and took the plunge.

There was Mary, all right. Big brown eyes. Wavy brown hair. Enormous smile. A clear reflection of the little girl she'd been. Leaping into the air the way Keely had seen her do so many times when she'd been cheerleading at high-school football games and basketball games and track meets. So many times when Keely had been sitting in the bleachers with no one at all to share the experience, the pleasure with…

She put that picture behind the others and looked at the next one.

Mary in her nightgown, striking a pose as if her bedroom were the prize display on a game show.

Again Keely suffered the memory of more evenings than she could count alone with Mary, then all alone after Mary had gone to bed, doing nothing but sitting in front of the television until Keely went to bed herself.…

That photograph went behind the first and Keely stared at the last of them.

Mary was standing in front of the apartment building with the two friends she was sharing the new place with. Katie Wurtz and Karen Stieger.

Keely had to smile at the sight of the three girls who had been friends since grade school, all grown up. All grown up and on their own, not needing the kind of care they'd needed before, making their caregivers obsolete.

Keely pressed the pictures to her chest and closed her eyes.

''Okay. I get it,'' she said, as if it had been someone else presenting the case against potentially allowing history to repeat itself with Devon Tarlington and Harley.

She left the bathroom and went across the hall to her bedroom where she stashed the photographs in her drawer.

The problem was, the minute they were out of sight, the image of Devon replaced them in her mind's eye. Tall, muscular, handsome, sexy Devon Tarlington.

Devon who made her laugh. Who made her feel better than anyone had in so, so long. Who made her feel like a living, breathing, attractive, desirable woman again.

And even though she knew she should be making up her mind not to go to Dunbar with him, not to see him again unless she needed to give Harley to him, even though she knew that was the only way to really keep herself—her heart—safe, making that decision felt bad. And because it felt bad, it didn't feel like the right choice. After all, shouldn't the right choice feel good and the *wrong* choice feel bad?

That seemed only logical.

"And you're just trying to talk yourself out of what you know you should do and into what you know you shouldn't do," she chastised herself as she climbed into her bed with a stack of magazines she'd planned to catch up on.

And that was when something else struck her. Something big.

The wedding was on Saturday and it was nearly eleven o'clock Friday night.

Eleven o'clock Friday night and Devon hadn't called her as he'd said he would to find out whether she wanted to go or not.

So maybe the decision had already been made for her.

* * *

"Hey! Where are you? You look like you're a million miles away."

Devon was sitting at the bar of the brew pub he and Ethan had taken over for Aiden's bachelor party when Aiden joined him.

"Just enjoying my buzz," Devon lied. The truth was that his mind *had* been a million miles away. Or at least a few blocks away. At Keely's house. But he wasn't going to admit that.

Apparently he didn't have to, though, because Aiden said, "I'll bet you were daydreaming about Keely."

"Nah, I'm telling you, it's just the buzz," Devon insisted.

"You know, by this time tomorrow night I'll be all married up. Two down, one to go," Aiden said pointedly.

Devon laughed. "How about two down and we're done with weddings?"

Aiden sat on the bar stool beside Devon. "We all liked Keely. A lot."

"Oh, that was subtle," Devon said, laughing again at his brother's meddling.

"We did," Aiden insisted. "She fit right in."

"Uh-huh," Devon said noncommittally.

"She'd be good for you."

Devon merely rolled his eyes at that one.

"Last night with all of us together, with all three babies, it was really nice," Aiden persisted.

Devon took a drink of his beer and scanned the crowd.

"You could do worse," his brother pointed out.

Devon laughed yet again, wryly this time. "I *have* done worse."

"I'm just saying—"

"I know what you're just saying and quit saying it. Quit *thinking* it," Devon ordered.

But Aiden ignored the command. "Right, because you're not warm for her form at all," he said sarcastically—and a bit thickly. "That's why you hardly took your eyes off her the whole night last night."

"I think all this beer has you hallucinating in retrospect," Devon joked.

But his brother didn't let him get away with it. "Right. And I suppose the reason you called other people by Keely's name three times today was because you weren't thinking about her at all, huh?"

"I didn't do that," Devon said, knowing full well that he had.

Aiden didn't argue, he only smiled a knowing smile and took a drink of his beer before he said, "So, is she coming to the wedding?"

Devon shrugged. "I don't know," he said as if it didn't matter to him one way or the other.

"*Shouldn't* you know? Wouldn't she be coming with you?"

"She said last night that she had to think about it."

"You mean *you* couldn't persuade her to jump right in?" Aiden goaded. "You must be losing your touch."

"I must be," Devon agreed.

"And she didn't let you know today?"

"Actually, I was supposed to call her," Devon admitted, somewhat under his breath because it was an issue he'd been grappling with since he'd rolled out of bed after a nearly sleepless night.

But Aiden heard him anyway. He looked at his watch. "The day's almost over. You're a little late."

Maybe too late...

But Devon was spared having to respond to that as one of Aiden's old medical-school buddies stood on a table to make a toast.

Not that Devon heard much of the teasing that went along with it because it was Keely who was still on his mind. Keely and the fact that he'd told her he'd call and he hadn't.

Sure, he'd been busy. With wedding stuff. With family stuff. With party stuff. But he could have spared a few minutes for a phone call.

And why hadn't he?

Because of what was eating at him.

He hadn't called Keely because he'd wanted to hear her say that, yes, she would go with him to Dunbar.

He'd wanted to hear it *too* much.

And that was somehow worse than only being afraid she'd say no. That made it seem as if he already had too much invested. And worrying about that had kept him away from the telephone.

He was still on the fence when it came to Harley, still full of doubts about his ability to be a dad if it turned out he was the baby's father, still not happy about the prospect. But when it came to Keely, something else was happening. And it was happening fast.

And the fact that he'd spent all of last night obsessing over how to convince her to come with him this weekend, the fact that her coming or not coming seemed like it would make or break the weekend for him, was weighing on his mind something fierce.

It just shouldn't have been that important to him. It had never been that important to him if another woman was with him for any other occasion. Why did it matter so much now? With *this* woman?

But in spite of asking himself those same questions all day long, he still didn't have any answers. And not being able to sort it out had only frustrated him further. It had made him disgusted with himself. And his only solution had been not to call her at all. Not to give in to what he wanted to do more than he should.

So, as a result, he still didn't know if her answer was yes or no.

And not knowing was still driving him crazy.

Maybe that was the real answer—he'd just lost his mind. Which, at that moment, didn't seem too far-fetched. And worst of all, he'd lost his mind over a woman who he believed was wrong for him.

There was just no denying that Keely was like Patty. Patty, who he'd hurt. Unintentionally. But he'd hurt her just the same. And he didn't ever want to do that again. He sure as hell didn't want to do it to

Keely. Which meant that he should nip things in the bud before this went any further.

And nipping things in the bud definitely wouldn't happen if she came to Dunbar this weekend.

So he should be hoping she'd decided not to. Even if it meant the weekend and the wedding would be ruined for him. Better that than things ending up the way they had with Patty.

Except that, try as he might, Devon couldn't seem to accept that.

"So, would you say I'm just a selfish bastard?" he asked Aiden when the toast was over and he had his brother's attention again.

Aiden laughed and looked confused. "Uh...was that what we were talking about before?"

"I'm just wondering. Would you consider me a selfish bastard?"

"No," Aiden answered without having to think about it. "And what brought that up?"

"Keely."

Aiden still looked confused. "Keely thinks you're a selfish bastard?"

"No. Am I a selfish bastard because I want to see her, I want to spend time with her, when I know it probably won't lead where she wants it to?"

"Where does she want it to lead?"

"I don't know. I just met her," Devon said as if his brother were dim.

"Maybe you should get to know her and *then* decide if you're on different tracks."

Devon knew he was a little drunk, and he wondered

if that was the only reason his brother's words made sense. But the more he thought about it, the more convinced he became that, drunk or sober, they *did* make sense.

"You're right. I don't know her all that well. And just because she seems more like Patty than Clarissa doesn't necessarily mean she *is* like Patty."

"She seemed like herself to me," Aiden said.

Devon laughed. "Whatever *that* means. I think you're getting plastered."

Aiden grinned a silly grin that confirmed it.

But what his brother had said about getting to know Keely did seem reasonable to Devon. No one could get hurt just by doing that, could they?

And what better way to really get to know each other than to have this weekend in Dunbar?

Not to mention that maybe that's why he wanted her to be there so much—he just wanted to get to know her.

Devon threw back the last of his beer and set his glass on the bar.

"Refill?" the bartender asked.

"No thanks," Devon declined, because suddenly it seemed that the vow he'd made that morning to prove he could control himself on the Keely front, to prove he had willpower when it came to her, to prove that whether she went to Dunbar was no big deal to him, to prove all these things by putting off calling her until Saturday morning, was just silly.

In fact, he no longer even saw the point in talking to her over the phone.

Not when her house was only a short distance away.

* * *

By midnight Keely had gone from indecision to downright dejection and depression. Obviously Devon wasn't going to call. Probably he'd reconsidered the idea of spending the weekend with her and changed his mind. Or maybe he'd just hooked up with a bridesmaid today, someone who didn't represent a woman he'd been involved with who had been involved with someone else at the same time. Someone who wasn't on the cusp of possibly altering his whole life in a way he wasn't happy about.

Not that Keely didn't believe it was for the best if Devon's interests were on someone other than her. She figured she'd been saved from herself and her own weakness for a man she should steer very, very clear of.

It was just that she didn't appreciate that it hadn't been her own choice. She didn't like feeling rejected. Or discarded.

Or jealous.

No, she *really* didn't like feeling jealous.

Jealous, of all things. And for nothing more than *imagining* that Devon hadn't called because he might have met someone else.

This was getting out of hand, she told herself. Ridiculously out of hand. So it was good that at least one of them was putting a stop to it. And now that Devon had, and she wouldn't be spending the weekend with him, she'd spend it tracking down the other guy who might be Harley's dad and get closer to putting this whole thing to an end.

Which was exactly how it should be.

A little *ping* pulled her out of her own reverie. A little *ping* on her window.

Keely's thoughts stopped whirling long enough to wonder what that had been. She turned her head on the pillow to look in the direction from which the sound had come, even though she couldn't see through the drawn curtains.

Her room was on the second floor. Not a likely place for a pebble from a passing car tire to have hit. Or anything else for that matter. Unless the wind was blowing hard, and as far as she could tell there wasn't even a breeze.

Ping!

There it was again.

She swung her legs out of bed and padded barefoot to the window without turning on a light.

Ping! Ping!

Her window faced the street, and she began to wonder if there were some neighborhood kids outside, starting their Halloween pranks early this year. If they knew what was good for them they'd run, because Keely was in just enough of a bad mood to make them sorry they'd picked this place to throw rocks at.

Ping!

Oh, you're really going to get it, whoever you are.

She flung the curtains wide just as a tiny rock hit the glass. Without so much as a glance outside first, she slid the lower pane up and poked her head out the screenless opening.

Just in time to get hit in the forehead by the latest rocket launch.

"Ouch!"

"Whoops."

She knew who that voice belonged to, and it was enough—even after being hit with a rock—to chase away every rotten feeling she'd suffered in the last hour. To lift her spirits just that quickly. Just that easily.

"Devon?" she said, trying to keep her voice quiet so as not to wake anyone.

"Yo," he said by way of answering, but it came out a singsong.

It took her a moment to pinpoint where he was, but she finally spotted him in the shadows between the two ancient elm trees in her front yard.

"What are you doing out there?" she asked in a quiet voice.

"I came to see you," he said simply and not quietly at all. "I thought maybe I could get you to take a midnight walk with me."

"Do you know what time it is?"

"Midnight. When else could we take a midnight walk?"

Keely saw a light go on in the house across the street and she knew he'd awakened old Mrs. Black. Old Mrs. Black who could be a big pain in the neck when she got in a snit.

Keely lowered her own voice even more and said, "Shh, we're waking the neighbors."

"Then come down so we don't have to holler back and forth," he suggested loudly.

"Okay, okay. Just be quiet. It'll take me a minute to get dressed and then I'll be there."

"Hurry."

That had been easy for him, hadn't it? she thought as she closed the window and rushed to her closet for clothes. He hadn't called the way he'd said he would, then he showed up unannounced in the middle of the night to throw rocks at her window like a bad kid, and here she was rushing into a turtleneck sweater and a pair of jeans as fast as she possibly could. Plus, if that wasn't enough, she also yanked the scrunchie out of her hair, flipped over so her head was upside down and she could finger-comb her curls, then swiped on mascara, too. She was acting as if she was so thrilled to see him that nothing else mattered.

Of course she *was* thrilled to see him and nothing else *did* matter, but she knew that shouldn't have been the case.

"You're in deep trouble," she told her reflection when she took a quick look to make sure she was presentable.

But at that moment she just couldn't make herself care about anything other than the fact that Devon was outside waiting for her and she was going to get to see him today after all.

She snatched up a jean jacket to put on as she bounded down the stairs and out the front door, feeling like a kid herself, sneaking out of the house late at night to meet a boy.

But Devon was so much more than a boy.

Tall and striking, he was standing with his back against one of the trees by then, a khaki-clad leg bent at the knee so that the sole of his shoe was flat against the trunk.

He had on a sweater-knit polo shirt under a wool blazer, his arms were crossed over his chest and he was grinning a wicked grin that said he was very pleased with himself because he'd gotten her out there.

"The bachelor party must have been a bust," she said as if that were the only explanation for his visit.

"Actually, it was a huge success."

"And it's over already?" she persisted skeptically.

"Nope. It's still going strong."

"Then what are you doing here?" she asked, much as she had from her bedroom window.

He just grinned again, his eyes seeming to devour her.

Or maybe she was just projecting what she felt— the hunger to see him, to be with him, as if they'd been apart far longer than a single day.

Still, it crossed Keely's mind that whatever it was she saw in his eyes might not be reliable because she wasn't sure he was completely sober.

In an attempt to ascertain that she glanced at the curb and said, "Did you drive over?"

"Nope," he repeated with a kind of glee that said

he was enjoying saying the word itself. "We confiscated all the car keys at the door."

Which still didn't tell her whether or not he was three sheets to the wind. But that idea was gaining some ground the more he talked because he sounded so mellow.

He pushed off the tree and came near enough to bend over and study her forehead in the moon glow. "Did I really bean you?" he asked, sounding more amused by that notion than remorseful.

"Yes, you did."

Without warning he rubbed a big thumb over the spot, tracing it gently and setting off a little rain of sparkles through her.

"Let me kiss it and make it better," he said, doing exactly that before she even realized he was going to.

The feel of his lips against her skin added brightness to those sparkles he'd already kicked up and flooded her with the urge to tip her chin, to catch his mouth with hers and turn the kiss-to-make-it-better into the real thing.

But she resisted the inclination.

Then he raised his head just enough to nuzzle the top of hers with his nose and said, "God, I love the smell of your hair."

And that was when she became reasonably sure he wasn't in complete command of his faculties.

"Oh yeah, I think you're a little drunk," she said.

He straightened up and smiled down at her. "Maybe just a little." Then he pointed with his chin to her forehead. "But you feel better, don't you?"

"Oh, no doubt about it," she answered with a laugh. "I understand a kiss on the forehead is the cure for all concussions."

The full grin made another reappearance. "I didn't hit you that hard. I know because I was being careful not to break the window. But I am sorry," he finished, clearly only pretending contrition. And not doing it very well.

"You don't sound too sorry," Keely pointed out.

"Well, I am sorry I hit you. But I'm not sorry it got you down here."

"And why did you get me down here when you're supposed to be at your brother's bachelor party?"

He shrugged elaborately. "I just wanted to see you. Didn't you want to see me?"

There was no way she was admitting that. At least not so that it sounded as if she had. "More than I've ever wanted anything in my life—food, water, air, even chocolate."

But he seemed to miss the fact that she was being facetious because he grinned even bigger and said, "Good, because that's how much I wanted to see you."

Keely couldn't help laughing. "Just how drunk are you?" she asked, as if that explained the response that had pleased her more than she wanted to acknowledge.

"I'd still feel pain if you wanted to throw a rock at me to make us even," he informed.

"I'm not so sure about that," she said.

"Honest," he insisted. Then he nodded toward the

street. "Come on. Let's take our walk and you'll see I can still do it in a straight line."

He reached for her hand as if he had every right to, holding it as he led her to the sidewalk. And while Keely was sure she should have pulled out of his grip, she liked having that strong, powerful mitt wrapped around hers too much to deny herself.

So, instead, she held his hand in return and pretended it didn't mean anything, that it was nothing more than a friendly gesture and the most natural thing in the world.

The day had been particularly warm and although the temperature had cooled, it was still a wonderfully comfortable night to be out. The sky was clear and full of stars, and the moon cast a bright silver light as they began a leisurely stroll.

"Did you grow up around here?" Devon asked then, his deep voice enticing in the silence of the sleeping neighborhood.

It wasn't an unusual question, but the way it came out gave Keely the impression that it carried some weight for Devon. Although that didn't make much sense.

"I grew up a few blocks from here," she said.

"Is that where your parents are now? A few blocks from here?"

"Actually it was my grandmother's house and she passed away about seven years ago."

"You lived with your grandmother?" he asked, sounding as if that was a revelation.

Keely chuckled and looked at him out of the corner

of her eye. "Are you hanging on my every word for a reason?"

He cast her a smile that made it seem as though she'd found him out. "I just want to get to know you."

How could she find fault with that?

She couldn't, so she obliged him. "My grandmother raised my sister and me."

"Where were your parents?"

Keely shrugged. "Not around," she said with a measure of sadness in her voice. "I guess, really, they were sort of like Clarissa in the responsibility department. My mother got pregnant with me when she and my father were only sixteen. My father's parents were staunchly religious and insisted they get married. Then I was born and apparently they still weren't thinking about birth control—or doctor's orders, since you're not even supposed to have sex again for six weeks—"

"They were teenagers," Devon reminded her.

"Right. Fertile teenagers, because my mother was pregnant again with Hill before I was even a month old."

"You and your sister are only ten months apart?"

"We are."

"So your parents were what? Seventeen and they had two kids?"

"Seventeen, married, with two kids, no money and realizing rapidly that they weren't as wild for each other as they had been when they'd started going steady."

"Oh, man, that's a recipe for disaster if I've ever heard one," Devon groaned.

"Mmm," Keely agreed. "My father's family moved out of the state not long after the wedding—they considered themselves disgraced—and my grandfather on my mother's side had died in a bus accident. So that left my grandmother on my mother's side as the only one to help my parents. She did all she could, but it didn't make any difference. Before I was two years old my father couldn't deal with it anymore, and he decided to join the army. Grams said he told her it was so he'd have a future, but really it was just a sanctioned way to bail out. My mother wasn't letting him get away that easily. She announced that she was going with him."

"Was she welcome to?"

"Grams said there was a lot of fighting, but in the end the plan was for my mother to go wherever my father was stationed—leaving Hillary and me with Grams. Then, as soon as they were settled on an army base, they'd send for us."

"But that didn't happen," Devon supplied.

"Not quite. About a month later my mom sent Grams a letter saying that they were splitting up, that neither of them wanted us and that Grams could put us up for adoption."

"They were a *lot* like Clarissa," he commented.

"Anyway," Keely continued, "Grams adopted us and raised us herself."

"And your parents?"

"No one ever heard from either of them again.

Grams or Hill or I could have traced our father through the military, but none of us saw the point. For whatever reason—immaturity or fear or selfishness or irresponsibility—they both opted completely out of our lives and…I don't know…maybe we all just felt the same way—that if they wanted back in they'd show up. And if not, it wouldn't do any good to track them down."

"But in the meantime, you and your sister stayed within blocks of where they left you so you wouldn't be too hard to find."

That insight surprised Keely, and she glanced up at him. "You know, I never thought of it like that. We haven't ever really gone far from home. I wonder if, subconsciously, that's partly why. We've always just figured this was home to us, but I know we've also talked about our parents looking us up someday. Maybe somewhere in our psyches we've stayed close to where they left us so they'd know where to look."

"What happened to your grandmother?" Devon asked as they rounded the block and headed back toward Keely's house.

"She's actually the reason Hill and I started Where Are They Now? Grams had a rare blood disease that took its toll on just about every organ of her body. The last year of her life she needed constant care. That was when Hillary and I came up with a way to be self-employed and work out of the house so she wouldn't have to go to a nursing home. When she died we had to sell the place to pay the medical bills. But by then we were really enjoying the people-finding business, so we decided to keep at it."

"And then eventually you bought the house you're in now—"

"Well, not then, no," she said, avoiding the story of what *had* happened because she wasn't ready to go into it. "We weren't doing enough business to buy the house until about a year ago. And we bought one only a few blocks from where we grew up because maybe we're a little nuts," she joked to distract him from that gap in the timeline.

"And that's how you ended up with Clarissa and Harley," he finished for her. Then he leaned sideways and nudged her with his shoulder. "And I wasn't saying you were nuts because maybe somewhere deep down you're hoping your parents will find you here," he added. "I was just making an observation. If there was any chance of my brothers and me ever having our parents back we'd probably live on the moon to accomplish it."

Keely thought that was a nice thing to say and it only made her like him even more.

They were back where they'd started and they went all the way up onto her porch as if he'd brought her home at the end of a date.

That was when he said, "I was supposed to call you today."

"Did you?" she asked as if she simply might have missed it if he had and one way or another she hadn't given it a second thought.

"No, I didn't."

"You said you were going to be busy today," she reminded, giving him an out.

"I was. But that isn't why I didn't call."

Keely gave him a sideways glance. "Are you fishing around for me to ask why?"

"Yes."

"Okay. Why didn't you call me today?"

"Because I was too afraid."

"Telephone phobia?" she joked.

They were standing at her front door and he was looking down into her eyes again. And even though he smiled at her jest, he was so intent on whatever it was he wanted to say that it didn't allow for much levity.

"I was too afraid you were going to say you wouldn't go to Dunbar with me, and I just didn't think I could handle hearing the no."

"Because women so rarely say it to you?" she asked, again joking. Partially, anyway.

"Because I didn't want to hear it from you. And because if you said it—if you say it now—the weekend won't be the same for me."

Oh, but the man's effect on her was potent! Keely actually felt her knees weaken, her heart beat faster— and her resolutions waver.

"I really should try to get a face-to-face meeting with Brian Rooney this weekend. I found out where he is today."

"Where?"

"Someplace on the eastern border of Colorado called Ryland. I've never heard of it but—"

"I know it. I've been there. In fact," he said with a hint of mischief in his eyes that let her know he was still slightly on the inebriated side, "you'd have to drive right through Dunbar to get there. So we could go to the wedding tomorrow, leave Harley with the nanny on Sunday and hit Ryland together, too.''

"You make that sound like a pleasure trip."

"Only because of the company I'd be keeping," he said with a glint in his eyes that made it all the more tempting to agree.

But she had to keep in mind that Brian Rooney was the third side of the triangle that had produced Harley and she still wasn't sure how wise it was to allow Brian Rooney and Devon to meet up.

Apparently he saw her hesitancy. "Okay, how about this—say you'll come to Dunbar and to the wedding with me tomorrow. Then you'll have another day to think about whether or not I can go with you to Ryland, and if you decide you don't want me to, I'll wait with Harley in Dunbar until you've done the deed."

That didn't seem like a bad idea. The weekend wouldn't go by without her making progress on Harley's behalf the way she'd decided she should, and she would still get to go to the Tarlington wedding.

All in all, a reasonable compromise. And if there were a lot of reasons why she'd been telling herself she *shouldn't* go to Dunbar and the wedding? At that moment, standing at her front door, looking up into Devon's jaw-droppingly handsome face, she couldn't recall any of them.

"Okay," she heard herself say, even as she considered the fact that maybe she should *make* herself recall the reasons.

But it was too late by then. Devon was grinning at her once more and seemed to emit a heat that wrapped around her like a cocoon and made her less willing to explore the negatives.

"Perfect," he said quietly.

Keely couldn't think of a response to that. But it didn't really seem as if she needed to make one as he went on delving into her eyes with his.

He took her right hand then, holding it just the way he was holding the left, and with his eyes still steady on hers, he moved closer. Closer. Until he dipped just enough to touch his mouth to hers.

It was a soft, parted-lips kiss that tested, that barely let her feel the warmth, the wonder, before it ended and he looked into her eyes again.

But if he was waiting for a complaint it didn't come from Keely. She only returned that piercing gaze, hoping tonight wouldn't be like the last night when a brief peck was the furthest he wanted to venture.

Maybe he really could read her thoughts because he did kiss her again. Less softly this time. More in command. More sure of what he wanted. Of the fact that she wanted it, too.

And she *did* want it, too. So much so that she abandoned one of his hands to answer an instinct, an urge, to touch him. To rest a palm along the side of his neck. His strong, corded neck.

He let go of her other hand and brought both of his to the sides of her waist. Gentle hands that relit those sparkling things inside her as his mouth continued moving over hers in a languid, sexy kiss that kept the promise that brief buss of the night before had made.

Even this was over too quickly for Keely as Devon

relapsed into studying her again, this time with a bad-boy smile.

"Oh no you don't," he said then, as if Keely had something up her sleeve, and he wasn't going to let her get away with it. "Too much of this and you'll say you won't go with me tomorrow because I have ulterior motives."

"Do you have ulterior motives?"

"Yes," he admitted, sounding less than sober again. Until he added, "But my ulterior motives aren't what you think."

"What are they?"

"I just want the time with you."

He said that in a quiet, sincere voice before he kissed her once more, quickly, and left her standing there on her porch as he did a little hop down the stairs.

"Noon. I'll be here at noon," he informed her as he left her there and disappeared into the night.

Keely had no choice but to go inside, to return to her bed, to try to get some sleep.

Which was no easier now than it had been earlier.

Although now dejection and depression and jealousy had nothing to do with it.

Now what kept her awake was reliving that kiss she knew she'd had no business liking as much as she had.

That kiss she certainly had no business wanting repeated when they were together in Dunbar.

Chapter Six

"Uh, Keely? Were you expecting a limousine?"

Keely was in her bedroom, closing her suitcase the next day when her sister hollered up from the entryway.

"A limousine? No," she called back.

"A big, black, stretch limousine," Hillary described. Then she added, "Oh, and there's Devon's SUV pulling up, too. What is this, a whole entourage?"

After making sure she had everything, Keely took her suitcase and headed down the stairs.

Hillary was sitting on the bottom step with Harley in her lap, putting on his coat. The front door was open so she could watch for Devon as Keely had asked her to.

By the time Keely had gone around her sister and Harley to set her suitcase beside the diaper bag and duffel bag she'd packed for the baby, Devon was coming up the walk and onto the porch.

Keely pushed open the screen and returned his simple, "Hi," but there was more of a questioning note in her voice as she glanced around him at what her sister had referred to as an entourage.

"Is there a parade to Dunbar?" she asked then.

Devon laughed. "Pretty much. We had to keep the bride and groom from seeing each other before the wedding so we decided women and children should go in the limo and men should follow behind in my car. Unless you want to ride with my brothers and me."

"And pass up a limousine? Not on your life," Keely responded, making it sound ridiculous that he'd even asked while in her heart of hearts she was disappointed that she and Harley wouldn't be alone with the big, handsome, jeans-and-sweater-clad man standing in her entryway.

"I'll just get you loaded up, then," he announced after saying hello to Hillary and giving a cursory wave to Harley. Then he picked up the suitcase, duffel and diaper bag and turned back to the door.

"I don't have a portable crib or anything for Harley," Keely said as she held the screen open for Devon. "Is that okay?"

"Ethan's already called ahead. There'll be three cribs in the nursery by the time we get there. Relax," he advised. "Everything is taken care of. Your job is just to have a good time."

He said that as he passed in front of her to get out, and as she watched him go down to the curb she thought that her job was really to not have too good a time. At least when it came to him. In fact, she'd given herself a stern talking-to that morning, and she'd vowed that in spite of attending his brother's wedding with him, in spite of staying at his brother's house with him, in spite of maybe allowing him to go with her to find Brian Rooney on Sunday, she would not allow things between them to go any further than they already had, and she swore she was sticking to it.

"Put your eyes back in your head, Keely, you're giving yourself away."

Keely hadn't heard her sister get up from the step to join her at the door, but there Hillary was, carrying Harley on one hip.

"I don't know what you're talking about," Keely said, tearing her gaze off Devon to look at the two of them.

"Right." Hillary smirked. "You could just jump his bones right here, couldn't you?"

"Shh!" Keely warned as if Devon might hear. "You couldn't be more off base. I was thinking that even though we'll be together for the next couple of days I will absolutely not let anything get out of hand."

Hillary laughed as if Keely had said something hilarious. But rather than address it, Hillary pressed her nose to the side of Harley's little head and said into his ear, "You better play chaperon this weekend. I think she needs one."

Keely just rolled her eyes and reached for the baby.

But the truth was, she did think of Harley as a chaperon. Harley and the rest of Devon's family. A whole slew of chaperons that would aid her cause.

It was just that when Devon came back to get her and put a hand at the small of her back to guide her to the waiting cars, that simple, innocent touch was enough to make her blood run quicker.

It was also enough to make her wonder if even a slew of chaperons would be enough.

Keely had never ridden in a limousine, so that was a new—and pleasant—experience. Especially when she shared it with Paris and Emmy, with whom she felt as comfortable as she did with her own sister.

They passed the time doing manicures while all three babies napped, talking about the wedding and the honeymoon trip Emmy and Aiden were taking to Brazil.

And then they arrived at Ethan and Paris's home.

It sat at the end of a mile-long drive lined on either side by red oak trees that grew together into a canopy overhead, a bright burnt-orange canopy, since the leaves had turned fiery in their autumn splendor.

For a moment, when the house came into sight behind the fountain made to look like water falling over a natural rock formation, Keely wondered if she'd misunderstood and the wedding was being held at a country club. Because while it might have been built of rustic logs, the two-story, U-shaped structure still had a refined air about it. Not to mention that it seemed at least the size of a full city block. But when Paris said, "Ah, home sweet home," Keely realized this wasn't the country club after all.

The limousine pulled up in front while Devon drove the SUV around the left side of the place and disappeared. By the time Keely, Paris and Emmy had unfastened car seats and gotten out themselves, Ethan and Devon had come through the front door to help.

Something about her expression must have alerted Devon to the things going through her mind because he leaned in close to her ear and whispered, "Pretty amazing, isn't it?"

Before she answered that, though, out came a woman with stark white hair, giving orders to Devon, Ethan and the limousine driver.

"This is Lolly McGinty," Devon told Keely. "She puts housekeeper on her tax returns, but the truth is she runs this place and everybody in it," he teased the older woman. "Lolly, this is Keely Gilhooley—honest, I didn't make up that name—and this is Harley."

The woman said she was pleased to meet Keely and didn't hesitate to come up and take a close look at Harley, who was just waking from his nap in the car seat Keely was holding.

"Harley, huh?" the housekeeper said to Devon as she took a long, close look at the baby. "I can see for myself that Clarissa's his mother, all right. But that's about it. Couldn't say one way or another whether there's you in him or Brian.''

So this woman knew the situation and Brian Rooney, too?

Keely's curiosity was piqued, but with so many people around she could hardly ask any of the questions the woman's comment had roused and instead found herself herded inside with everyone else.

The interior of the house was even more impressive than the exterior. The first floor held formal living and dining rooms, more casual breakfast and family rooms, a den, an enormous kitchen, a library, a movie theater and even a bowling alley and basketball court.

Upstairs there were eight bedrooms, complete with their own private baths, as well as two sitting rooms and a soundproof music studio that had been turned into the bride's dressing room.

Lolly and the woman introduced to Keely as Nellie, the nanny, carted Harley and the other babies off to the nursery. Ethan, Paris and Emmy scattered in different directions, too, leaving Devon to show Keely the room that would be hers.

''You're here and I'm there, right next door,'' he informed her as he opened the door and took her suitcase into the elegant space she'd been assigned. Then he added, ''Not too shabby, huh?''

''I think it'll do,'' she said in understatement as she looked over the four-poster bed, the Victorian bureau and dressing table, and the armoire that concealed a large television and stereo system.

Regardless of the luxury of her accommodations,

though, what she was really interested in was finding out how the housekeeper knew Brian Rooney.

But just as she was about to ask, Devon said, "I'm afraid I need to desert you."

"Oh, sure, lure me all the way to this remote location and then just dump me," she joked, fighting the second wave of disappointment that she was still not going to see much of him.

"It's all in my master plan," he played along. "Absence makes the heart grow fonder, remember?"

"Ah."

"No, actually Lolly says we have just enough time for showers and getting dressed. Then I should stick with Aiden until after the ceremony in case he needs moral support."

"There's no rest for the groomsmen," she pointed out. "So what does all this mean? I'll just see you at the reception?" She hadn't intended the growing disappointment to sound in her voice, but a bit of it had and she only hoped he hadn't heard it.

Apparently he had, because he gave her a devilish smile and said, "Can't live without me, huh?"

Keely laughed and shook her head as if he were completely out of his mind to think such a thing. "What an ego," she nearly groaned.

Devon was undaunted, though. He merely went on grinning at her as if he believed she couldn't live without him even if she did deny it.

Then he said, "The whole shindig will be in the heated tents out back and Lolly will make sure you and Harley get there, if that's okay with you."

"Sure, that's fine," Keely agreed.

"I promise, just as soon as the ceremony is over I won't leave your side for a minute the rest of the weekend," Devon said with more of that grin that seemed to raise the temperature in the room.

"It's all right," she assured him. "Really. You just do whatever you need to do, and we'll see you afterward."

But still Devon didn't rush out. He stayed there for a moment, studying her with a smile that had turned quiet and contemplative before he said, "Have I told you yet that I'm glad you came?"

"No, you haven't," Keely said as if it were an unforgivable oversight when in fact she wished he would stop saying things that reached that soft spot she had for him.

"Well, I am," he said in a quiet, very sexy voice. "How about you? Any regrets so far?"

"No regrets. So far," she answered, still trying to keep things light.

Not that she'd succeeded, however. Because the intimacy in his voice somehow echoed in hers.

And that was something she thought probably didn't bode well for keeping things between them from going any further than they already had.

A thought that was confirmed when Devon dipped in for a quick hit-and-run kiss before he left....

Keely wished her sister was with her to see the wedding of Aiden Tarlington and Emmy Harris. Even though Hillary's plans for a small, intimate wedding and reception couldn't compare, she knew her sister would have loved seeing it.

There were two white tents in the backyard, each of them the size of a football field. The ceremony was to be held in one and the formal, sit-down dinner would be served in the other while the first tent was reconfigured to accommodate dancing after the meal.

Hundreds of tiny white lights lined the insides of both tent tops, giving the illusion of stars. And in the first one, an archway of those same lights ran from the tent's opening all the way to the opposite end to mark the bride's walk up the aisle.

Wildflowers of deep purple, pink and yellow were strung in garlands all along the perimeter of the tent, as well as at the ends of each row of white chairs arranged for the guests. There were also wildflower garlands wrapped around and draped between the dozen columns that braced white candles in a semicircle behind the platform where the bride and groom would say their vows.

"This is just spectacular, isn't it?" Keely said to Lolly, who—good to Devon's word—had escorted Keely and Harley outside and was sitting with them in the front row.

"Ethan wanted no expense spared," the housekeeper said in response, her voice echoing with a maternal pride.

Hillary was to have a solo organist play the processional at her wedding, but here there was a quartet of violinists.

Paris was the matron of honor and she came down

the aisle pushing a very ornate antique baby carriage adorned with more wildflowers. The carriage was big enough to accommodate both Mickey—dressed in a tiny tuxedo—and Hannah, who had on an adorable dress the same deep-mauve color as the silk chemise her mother wore. Attached to the front of the baby carriage was a purple velvet pillow bearing the rings.

Emmy followed in a white gown with a beaded, formfitting bodice that met a full, floor-length skirt of iridescent satin. Her veil reached her elbows and was dotted with pearls that caught the glow of the lights and reflected it like moon glow on snow.

But despite the beauty of the bride, despite the elegance of the trio of tall, straight-backed Tarlington men, it was Devon who Keely had trouble tearing her eyes from.

Devon, who looked even more incredible in the tux than he did in the casual clothes she'd thought suited his untamed spirit. Devon, whose chiseled profile was flawless against the backdrop of candlelight. Devon, whose bones she did want to jump.

Not that she would.

She wouldn't.

She absolutely would not.

But seeing him up there, seeing that tuxedo caressing his big body, seeing the precise cut of his hair, the sharp angles of his strikingly handsome face, all while reliving that kiss they'd shared the previous evening, certainly put some truth to what her sister had accused her of earlier.

To thwart it, Keely forced herself to look away. To

pay attention to the ceremony. But by then it was too late. The desire had a hold on her and she knew she was in for the fight of her life tonight. A fight with herself and her own urges. But a fight she was determined to win.

There was just too much at stake for her not to.

Aiden and Emmy were pronounced man and wife, and, after receiving the congratulations of their guests, they moved to the second tent. There everyone drank champagne and dined on a seven-course meal while toasts—some serious, some touching and others teasing—provided entertainment.

Then the real party began in the original tent, where a full orchestra had been set up at one end of a dance floor surrounded by tables and chairs.

The nanny took all three babies into the house to be put to bed, and although Devon's attention had been taken up by friends and well-wishers until then, once the dancing started his focus turned completely to Keely.

They drank more of the champagne that flowed freely and danced almost every dance. And even when they sat out one or two, Devon stayed right by her side, fending off other men's requests to dance with Keely before she could say anything.

Not that Keely had any complaints. After hardly seeing him throughout the day and having to share him with so many people and activities much of the evening, it was nice to finally be with him.

Plus he was a great dancer, although, even if he'd been horrible at it she wouldn't have minded that, either. At least she was in his arms, pressed against that wondrous male body, his warm, strong hands on the bare skin of her back where the simple black, knee-length cocktail dress she wore dipped down to expose it.

She lost some of his attention at the end of the evening, after Aiden and Emmy had left the reception and it fell to Ethan and Devon to say good-night to the guests as they began to depart, too. But then everyone was gone and Ethan and Paris said good-night, and Keely was alone with Devon.

"There's a little left in this one," he said, holding up a bottle of champagne to show her. "Shall we have a last glass?"

It was well after midnight by then, and, although Keely was more sober than not, she didn't want to risk having one more drink that might dull her senses. Not when she was enjoying the sight of Devon looking so handsome in what remained of his tux once he'd discarded his coat, tie and cummerbund. Not when she could still smell a faint hint of his aftershave. Not when the sound of his voice was like dark, rich honey to her ears. And not when what she'd already had to drink might not have left her impaired but *had* seemed to weaken her defenses and her resolve. Defenses and resolve that might completely collapse with very little additional encouragement.

"No, no more for me to drink. I have a job to do tomorrow—I mean, today. Remember?"

"I do," he said, setting the bottle down without pouring himself another glass, either. "And besides,

I suppose we're in the way here,'' he added with a nod in the direction of the cleaning crew. ''I was just looking for a reason to keep you around a little longer.''

''Was I going somewhere?'' Keely joked, trying to tamp down on the pleasure his admission inspired in her.

''Maybe to bed. It's late.''

That was true. But it was also true that she wasn't inclined to end the evening yet.

She didn't want to admit that, so instead she said, ''I'm not tired. But we probably should at least get out of here.''

He agreed and they headed for the house.

She wondered if it was another side effect of all the champagne, but along the way it seemed perfectly natural for Devon to wrap his arm around her shoulders to keep her warm. Perfectly natural for her to lean into his side. To let her body drink in the heat of his.

''So what's your decision about tomorrow's venture?'' he asked as they went into the house, referring to whether or not she would let him go with her to find Brian Rooney.

''That's right, I was supposed to tell you that tonight, wasn't I?'' she said, not having thought much about it during the festivities.

''Yes, you were,'' he confirmed.

But in the quiet of the sleeping house their voices seemed loud and he came close to whisper, ''Let's go into the den where we won't wake anyone up.''

Keely nodded her agreement, noticing—but not regretting—that he didn't let go of her even though there was no longer a need to keep her warm.

A single green-glass-shaded lamp was lit on the desk in the den when they got there, and neither of them turned on any other lights. They just made their way to the leather couch and sat down, both of them in the center of the seat, close enough for Devon's shin to run the length of her thigh when he angled toward her, propped one ankle on the opposite knee, and stretched his arm along the sofa back just behind her.

Then, with his free hand, he took one of hers, holding it, smoothing his thick thumb against the back of it. "So what's it going to be?" he asked in a normal octave again now. "Can I keep you company when you go to Ryland to see Brian or not?"

It occurred to Keely that she finally had an opening to ask the questions she'd been wanting to ask since her arrival here, and she opted for seizing her opportunity.

So, rather than answering Devon's question, she tried what she hoped would be a segue. "I was surprised that Lolly knew about the situation and that she seemed to know Brian Rooney and Clarissa, too."

"I told you Brian and I are both from Dunbar, that we grew up together," Devon said, as if that explained it.

"Yes, I know you told me that. But why does that mean your brother's housekeeper seems to know so much about what's going on and about who Harley looks like?''

''Well, Lolly's a lot more than Ethan's housekeeper. She's lived in Dunbar all her life and she was one of the people who helped raise us. In fact, I'd say that of all the women who mothered us growing up, Lolly was the main mom. She was who we'd go to with problems even when we weren't staying with her.''

''And because she's always lived in Dunbar and Brian Rooney did, too, she knew him,'' Keely concluded.

''Right.''

''And she knows Clarissa, too?''

''Not from Clarissa having lived anywhere near Dunbar, but yes, she met her.'' Devon studied their clasped hands for a moment before he said, ''This is a pretty long tale of woe. Are you sure you want to hear it now?''

''I want to hear it if you want to tell it,'' she assured him, as if she hadn't done some tap-dancing to get them to that point. Then, as an added incentive, she said, ''Maybe it will help me make up my mind about you coming with me tomorrow.''

He grinned at her as if he'd seen through that ploy. ''Or maybe you're just blackmailing me for information.''

Keely smiled. ''Maybe.''

He laughed. ''Okay. But don't say I didn't give you fair warning.''

Still, he didn't seem to be in any hurry to get on

with it. He continued to stare at their hands, caressing hers with gentle, caring strokes.

"So Lolly knows Brian Rooney because she's always lived in Dunbar, and both you and Rooney grew up here," Keely reiterated to prompt him.

Another long moment passed as Devon seemed to refuse to be hurried. But then he finally said, "Before Ethan brought Tarlington Software to Dunbar, Dunbar was a much smaller town. Literally, everybody knew everybody else. Lolly was good friends with the Rooneys and she knew Brian almost as well as she knows me. In fact, since Brian was my best friend, when Lolly took her turn having my brothers and me stay with her family, Brian would be around as much as I would."

"When you told me you and Brian Rooney were both from Dunbar I wondered if that meant you were friends or acquaintances. If maybe all three of you had lived here and known each other, even just in passing. But you and Brian Rooney were *best* friends?"

"He was as close to me as my brothers," Devon confirmed.

"Was his family one of those you and your brothers stayed with?"

"It was. But Brian and I were friends even before my folks died. He lived next door to us, our parents were close, and Brian and I were the same age. There are pictures of us together as babies in diapers. Even when it came time to leave Dunbar for college, we went together. Then we shared a studio and a dark-room in Denver until the whole Clarissa thing.''

"I knew he was a photographer, too. I came across that information while I was looking for him."

"Not wildlife, though. He's a portrait photographer."

"So when, where and how did Clarissa come into the picture?'' Keely asked then. "No pun intended."

"When? Less than two years ago. Where? In a bar. In Denver. I don't suppose that comes as any surprise to you since you knew Clarissa, too, and how much she likes to party. And how? She actually fell into my lap. She was dancing on a table, slipped and I caught her. For a while I thought that was fortuitous,'' he finished with an edge to his voice.

"And was it love at first sight?"

"Infatuation at first sight is more like it,'' Devon said. "She was beautiful and spontaneous and full of life—things that seemed pretty exciting at the start. But later that all just translated to her being irresponsible and reckless."

"So Lolly met Clarissa when the two of you were together?'' Keely guessed.

"Right. I brought Clarissa here a few times. Clarissa, Brian and I came for Christmas that year."

"Did the three of you do a lot together?"

"Pretty much. Brian and I were close and, well, obviously so were Clarissa and I."

"But she was *with* you?"

"That's what I thought. For three months we were hot and heavy. Inseparable."

"And during that time she and Brian..."

"Were just cordial to each other. Or so I thought. The way I'd expect any woman I was serious with to be with my best friend or my brothers."

"And you didn't have any idea something more was developing?" Keely asked, having difficulty believing Clarissa—or any woman—would cheat on a man like Devon.

"Believe me, I've gone over it in my mind a million times. But no, I didn't see any signs that anything was happening between them. As far as I knew, they never even saw each other unless I was with them."

"And you really cared for Clarissa?" Keely wasn't eager to hear the answer to that but something drove her to ask anyway.

"I was in love with her," Devon said frankly, as if it was far enough in the past to make it easy for him to admit. "And as for Brian—never in a million years would I have expected him to knife me in the back like that."

"How did you find out they were more than...cordial?" Keely finally asked straight-out.

But apparently not even time and distance helped blunt the feelings that question brought to the surface, because for a moment he just stared down at their hands again while a muscle flexed in his jaw.

"It's okay if you don't want to tell me," she said, although if he didn't she thought she might die of curiosity.

Devon shook his head as if he still couldn't quite believe the culmination of events, but he finally said,

"I came home from a shoot in New Zealand a day early and found them in bed together. At my house. In my bed."

"People have been known to commit rash acts under circumstances like that."

"Yeah, it wasn't the best experience of my life to find the woman I loved in bed with my best friend."

"What did you do?"

"I got a little mad," he said in understatement with a wry laugh. "I threw some things—including a few punches at Brian. I did some screaming. Some pretty colorful cussing. About what you'd expect, I guess. The whole thing was like some bad soap opera, and I suppose so was my response."

"It's the double whammy—being betrayed by both the woman you love *and* your best friend."

"Definitely the double whammy," he agreed.

"And then what happened?"

"I kicked them both out of my house and that was the last I saw of Clarissa."

"But not of Brian?"

"He called a couple of times, came around once, trying to tell me that it wasn't his fault, that she'd seduced him, but that just didn't fly with me."

"You didn't believe him?"

Devon shrugged one of those wide shoulders. "It didn't much matter. Even if Clarissa did initiate it, if our positions had been reversed and Clarissa had been involved with Brian and come on to me? There's no way it would have worked. My biggest dilemma would have been how to tell him that was the kind of woman he was involved with. But by no stretch of the imagination would I have taken her to bed.''

Keely nodded, thinking that that made sense. ''And that was the last you saw or heard from Brian Rooney?''

''That was it.''

''But now you want to come with me to tell him about Harley?''

Once more Devon didn't plunge right into an answer. Only, rather than staring at their hands he raised his gaze to her hair, taking one of the free-falling curls to roll between his fingers as if it were a strand of silk.

This time Keely knew what he was really doing. She could see it in his face. He was getting a handle on the unpleasant emotions roused by those memories he'd just explored. And when he'd succeeded at that and could smile a small, sexy smile at her again, he said, ''I want to go with you anywhere.''

The man had charm, there was no denying it. But this was too important to let it go to her head. At least *too* much.

So Keely practiced some control of her own and said, ''I'm serious. The biggest fear Hillary and I have as people finders is that we're going to locate someone so the person looking for them can do them harm.''

Devon's smile broadened and looked genuinely amused. ''If I didn't blow Brian away the day I found him in my bed with Clarissa I'm not about to do it now. I told you why I want to go.''

"I know. So I won't have to spring the news of Harley on him alone. And just in case he does something stupid like refuse to give blood for the paternity test, you want to make sure he goes through with it since you have a high stake in this," she said, repeating almost verbatim what he'd told her at the start.

"And something about that seems unreasonable to you?"

"No," she admitted. "I just want the meeting to go smoothly and I'm not sure you being there will aid that."

"Actually, it might. Brian feels guilty about what he did to me but the last time I saw him he was still so resentful of Clarissa that he said he hoped he never had to see her or even hear her name again, that he didn't know what he might do if he did. So if you go to him alone, only on Clarissa's behalf, I'm afraid he might just tell you to go to hell. If I'm there to bring out some of the guilt he might be more likely to cooperate in order to make amends."

"Could he make amends? I mean, would you be open to patching up the friendship?" she said, testing.

"It'll never be the way it was before," Devon said. "I'm just saying that my being there could soften Brian's attitude."

"Or make it worse."

"Or make it worse," Devon conceded. "But how about this—if it looks at all like it's going in the wrong direction because I'm there, I'll leave." He paused a moment and then, as if to sweeten the pot, added, "And in the meantime, we can make a day of it. I can show you the scenic route to Ryland, we can go to a nice little restaurant I know of there. It won't seem so much like you're working on a Sunday."

Keely thought about all that. About the potential for a contrite Brian Rooney being more agreeable than a Brian Rooney who viewed her only as the delegate of the woman who had cost him his best friend. She thought about Devon's offer to leave them alone if his being there caused a problem. She also thought about how much she didn't want to face yet another stranger with shocking—and unwelcome—news, especially not alone. And about how nice it would be simply to make the trip with Devon, to turn the day into something more than a chore.

"Do you give me your word that you don't want to go just for the chance to punch him in the nose again?" she asked.

Devon laughed at that. "I give you my word."

"And if your being there makes things worse you'll get out and leave him to me?"

"Absolutely."

"Okay, then. But don't make me sorry."

His smile turned wicked and he leaned forward enough to rub her cheek with his chin. "I want to make you a lot of things, but sorry isn't one of them."

Keely laughed but it came out a bit breathy as the culmination of his effect on her washed through her and took over.

"Remember you promised to behave yourself,"

she said in an effort not to give in to those urges she'd
been battling all evening.

"I promised to behave myself *tomorrow*," he qualified, nuzzling her neck just a little.

Then he lifted his head and gazed into her eyes.
He brought her hand up to kiss the back of it before
he held it to his chest and took her mouth with his in
a kiss that was soft, alluring, playful.

But it wasn't long before the kiss deepened. Before
his lips parted and he kissed her in a way that made
the kisses they'd shared on previous occasions seem
like nothing at all.

He cupped her head in the hand that had been fid-
dling with her hair and moved her other hand so that
her palm was flat against his heart and he was free to
caress the column of her neck. Then his tongue introduced itself to the soft inner edges of her lips, to the
very tips of her teeth.

Keely knew this wasn't the smartest thing she'd
ever let happen. She knew she should stop him. But
oh, could the man kiss! And she was so instantly
caught up in it that she just couldn't make herself stop
it.

Instead she kissed him back. She let her lips part,
too, and when his tongue came to greet hers, she met
it with her own, answering in kind every circle, every
thrust, every parry, every game.

Her entire body seemed to be coming alive in response to him. To the touch of his hands. To the
sweet taste of his mouth. To the arousing dance of
that kiss. To finally having what it seemed she'd been

wanting every minute since he'd stopped kissing her the night before.

She felt her nipples harden, felt their cry for attention and, in response, she wrapped her arms around him so she could move closer into him. Close enough for her breasts to reach the hard, honed wall of his pectorals.

His hand at her neck left to find the middle of her back, to knead it, to massage it, to hold her even closer to him. So close that she wondered if he could feel the taut crests of her breasts against him, if that contact tantalized him the way it tantalized her.

But just when Keely was on the verge of taking a deep breath that would press her breasts even more firmly to him, to let him know she wanted this to go further, he began a sort of retreat. His tongue did one bold thrust and then pulled out. The wide-open kiss became slow, shorter kisses that weren't all on her lips, some went to her nose, her chin, her neck, before he stopped altogether and instead laid his brow to the top of her head.

"I'd like this to continue," he confessed then in a husky voice that relayed as much of the message as his words. "But if it does…"

"It might be a mistake," Keely finished, not sure if that was what he was going to say, but knowing that was what the little voice of caution in her own head was telling her.

"Okay," he said with a slight chuckle that told her that *hadn't* been how he was going to end that statement.

But if not, then how? Had he been about to say that if the kiss went on, he wanted it to go all the way? And here she'd jumped the gun and said it would be a mistake.

Keely wanted to kick herself.

Or at least a part of her did.

Another part of her thought better of it and realized that it was probably for the best that she never know what he'd had in mind. After all, she might have been too inclined to agree with it. Or to agree to it. And she thought that now that they had interrupted what was happening, it was best if it was left that way.

"Tomorrow will be a big day," she said as if that was why they should practice some restraint.

Devon raised his head from hers and looked into her eyes, smiling a half smile now. "The opening-their-gifts-brunch for Aiden and Emmy, and then to Ryland to find Brian," he outlined as if to let her know he remembered.

"So we should call it a night."

"We should," he said as if that didn't mean he was willing to.

Then he kissed her again. A simple kiss, unlike the one they'd just nearly been swept away by. And yet it was enough to weaken Keely's will even more.

But weak or not, she knew she had to resist him and this time she ended the kiss.

"I have to go," she informed him.

Then she made a liar out of herself by kissing him again.

But only once before she put both palms to his chest and pushed. "Really," she said.

Devon smiled again and nodded, this time with acceptance. "Whatever you say."

"I say it's probably better if you don't walk me to my room, either," she told him, knowing that would be a prime spot for another kiss. A prime spot right outside her bedroom. Or his...

This time his smile said he definitely knew what she was thinking. But he honored her wishes and spread his arms wide to get them completely away from her. "Whatever you say," he repeated as if he found this all funny now.

But Keely knew what was going through her own mind, her own body, too well not to make her getaway while she still had the strength. So she stood and went to the den's door before she turned to look at Devon again.

"Good night," she said, longing terribly to be back on that sofa with him, in his arms, kissing him, finding out what would have happened if they hadn't stopped.

"See you in the morning," he said.

But she went on lingering at that door. There was just something in those denim-blue eyes, something in that chiseled face, something about that big, masculine body, that made it so difficult for her to leave, to deny herself what every inch of her was urging her to go back to.

But she didn't do it.

She let herself have just one more moment of

standing there, drinking in the sight of him, longing for him—and then she finally made herself walk out of that room. Made herself walk down the hallway to her bedroom where she went inside and closed the door firmly behind her.

But even the confines of that pristine Victorian space didn't help chase away the longing.

Keely wasn't too sure if anything could. Anything short of having it satisfied.

Chapter Seven

When the knock sounded on Devon's bedroom door at seven the next morning he was asleep. Dead asleep. After all, he'd been up late the night before with Keely. And later still because even once she'd left him he hadn't been able to get her out of his head— or out of his system—enough to rest. So that first knock barely registered and it definitely didn't get a response from him.

He ignored the second knock, too.

But by the third it occurred to him that it might be Keely standing outside the door, rapping on it.

And that was enough to rouse him.

He rolled onto his back, stretched, crossed his arms under his head and said, ''Yeah. Come on in.''

But it wasn't Keely who opened the door.

It was Ethan.

Ethan carrying Harley.

"Morning," Devon's eldest brother said as he came in.

"Is something wrong?" Devon asked rather than answering the greeting, wondering if a problem with the baby had inspired this just-past-dawn appearance.

"No, nothing's wrong," Ethan said, crossing the room to Devon's bedside. "But I'm glad to see you care."

Devon still didn't understand what had prompted this visit and, as if to better get a grip on it, he pushed himself to sit up against the headboard, exposing his bare chest to the cooler air outside the blanket. "So what's going on?" he asked then, sounding as baffled as he felt.

"Paris and I have Hannah," Ethan explained simply enough. "Aiden and Emmy have Mickey. We thought you could take care of Harley for a while so the nanny could drink her coffee in peace. And so you could get some experience with our boy here. Just in case."

"You have to be kidding." And Devon honestly believed he was.

But Ethan wasn't. "No kidding," Ethan answered, holding out Harley for Devon to take.

Only Devon *didn't* take him.

Instead he put his hands up—palms outward—and refused. "Oh, no."

"Oh, yeah," Ethan countered. Then he bypassed

Devon to lie Harley beside him, braced on the extra pillow.

"Don't do this, Ethan," Devon said, staring daggers at his brother.

But Ethan didn't pay any attention to either the command or the glare.

What he did do was take a bottle out of the pocket of his robe to set on the nightstand.

Then he said, "Harley's had some fruit and cereal but he still needs his bottle. I wouldn't wait too long to give it to him. That pacifier isn't going to keep him quiet forever when he needs to finish his breakfast."

"I mean it, don't do this," Devon repeated.

"Too late. It's already done. Deal with it," the eldest Tarlington brother decreed with a satisfied smile as he walked out and closed the door behind himself.

"This isn't funny," Devon shouted after him.

"It's a little funny," Ethan called back through the door with unveiled amusement in his voice.

And there Devon was, alone with Harley.

And thinking, *Keely! I need Keely!*

Although this time that thought didn't have anything to do with the fact that he had the hots for her. This time it was pure desperation that brought her to mind. Desperation and the knowledge that if he could just get her in here, she would take care of Harley. That he wouldn't have to.

Of course if he did that he knew he'd never live it down with either of his brothers. That he'd forever be the one who'd been undone by a mere baby.

At the moment that seemed like the lesser of two evils.

Until he reconsidered.

Was he honestly going to drag Keely out of bed this early just because he couldn't handle giving a baby a bottle? A baby who wasn't hers, but who might be his?

What a lousy thing to do.

And if he actually got her in here, wasn't he going to sound like a jerk when he told her why? He was so scared of a baby who didn't even weigh as much as a Thanksgiving turkey that he hadn't been able to spend five minutes alone with him.

That was *not* how he wanted her to think of him.

And since he couldn't come up with a more viable—and face-saving—excuse, he was stuck. He couldn't call Keely to take care of Harley, and the nanny wasn't going to come to his rescue, either. He was on his own.

"Damn you, Ethan," he muttered under his breath, knowing that regardless of how much he didn't want to do this, he was going to have to.

Unless Harley just stayed lying on the pillow, sucking the pacifier, until the nanny finished her coffee....

With that thought and the hope that it might actually happen, Devon looked down at Harley. But only in a covert glance without moving so much as a muscle, as if complete stillness and not making eye contact might maintain the status quo and save him yet.

Harley was lying right where Ethan had left him. The infant was dressed in footed pajamas, his chubby hands were in fists near his cheeks, and he was staring up at Devon almost as warily as Devon was peeking at him. But he wasn't crying. He was merely sucking fiercely on that pacifier.

Great, just stay like that.

But no sooner had that silent plea run through Devon's mind than the sucking stopped.

Harley's brow wrinkled.

The corners of his mouth took a dive for his chin.

And Devon knew enough to sense a wail wasn't too far behind.

"No, you don't want to cry," Devon said as if that might forestall it, looking directly at the baby now.

But apparently Harley wanted to prove him wrong because, with that comment, the pacifier fell out of the infant's mouth and his bottom lip suddenly protruded in a mighty pout.

"Okay. You want your bottle? You can have it," Devon said, sounding more panicked than he had when the angry rhinoceros had charged camp in Africa two years ago.

He reached for the bottle Ethan had left on the night table and tried replacing the pacifier with that.

But Harley wouldn't take it. He just screwed up his face and let out a cry that started low and grew like a siren to alert someone that he'd been left in the hands of an incompetent. An incompetent he didn't want to be with.

"Yeah, I'm not any happier about this than you are," Devon informed him, wondering what the hell he was supposed to do now. "You can't need your diaper changed or Ethan would have brought one of those in, too. I'm sure that would have been even more entertaining for him than this. And you can't be tired because you just slept all night long. So it has to be food and here it is. Take it,'' he said, running through the list of possibilities Keely had outlined for him as the most common causes for babies to cry.

But reasoning with Harley didn't work. He still wasn't interested in the bottle.

''Come on, please, just take it,'' Devon urged.

Harley merely went on bawling.

Then it occurred to Devon that Keely usually held the infant to give him the bottle. He couldn't think why that should make any difference, but not knowing what else to try, he said, ''Is that what you want? Curb service isn't enough?''

Of course Harley didn't answer him. But Devon was willing to try anything, so he returned the bottle to the nightstand and reached for the baby.

''Oh, man,'' he groaned when he tried to grasp Harley under the arms and found the angle so awkward he was afraid he might break him if he actually lifted him like that.

And Harley wasn't all that eager either because he cried even harder, put one fist beside his mouth and turned his head in the opposite direction as if searching for help from another quarter.

''Okay, we'll try a different way,'' Devon said in an appeasing tone.

He slid one hand under Harley's rump and the

other under his head, managing to transfer the infant to lie across his legs.

But still Harley howled and refused the bottle.

"What do you want from me?" Devon asked, his own anxiety reaching new heights.

He had to admit that the baby didn't look too comfortable, though. And that this *wasn't* how Keely held him to feed him.

"It's going to be your way or no way, is that it?" he said.

But he conceded just the same and did his best to position the baby as he'd seen Keely do so many times. Against him. Resting Harley's head in the crook of his arm. Then he presented the bottle again.

Harley's cries became whimpers, but he still stared up at Devon as if Devon were some kind of monster.

"Come on, just eat. You'll feel better," Devon told him, offering the bottle once more.

And this time, to his surprise, Harley accepted it.

"Finally," Devon said, breathing a sigh of relief and thinking that he was going to plan something really big to get even with Ethan for this. Something huge.

"He might be enjoying his fun now, but I owe him one and I'm going to make him so sorry," Devon told the baby.

Although he had to admit that this wasn't *too* bad now. Harley had relaxed and was snuggling into him. Every muscle in Devon's body didn't feel tense anymore. And they suddenly seemed to be doing all right—to Devon's amazement.

"So. Here we are," he said to the baby lying innocently in his arms, staring back at him with big, round, trusting eyes.

Of course, Harley had no response to that. He merely went on drinking his bottle and watching Devon.

"You know, it's nothing personal," Devon continued. "My keeping my distance from you—that's nothing personal. I mean, you're a good enough baby. There's nothing wrong with you. Don't think any differently just because you had a mother who split and I'm kind of a doofus when it comes to you. Those are our problems. You're okay."

As if in answer, Harley raised a tiny hand toward Devon's face, even though it was out of the infant's short reach.

Devon felt sorry for him for the failed attempt and bent his head to accommodate the baby. Harley seized the opportunity and grabbed hold of his nose.

It made Devon laugh. "I'm having a life crisis here and you just want to see if the old schnozz honks," he said.

Then he straightened up again and Harley laid his palm against Devon's bare chest.

That tickled slightly and felt so odd that it drew his gaze. And that was when it struck him that it was such a tiny hand. So tiny it hardly seemed real. A tiny hand that belonged to a tiny person. A tiny, vulnerable person.

New emotions suddenly welled up in Devon, erasing his panic and frustration at being left with the baby, sobering his humor at Harley squeezing his nose.

"I'm sorry, Harley," Devon whispered, suddenly feeling very bad that Clarissa had left the baby without a backward glance. That he himself had been so unwilling to step up to the plate when it came to this child—this child who might be his.

"You didn't choose to be here, did you?" Devon asked. "You didn't ask to be born. And now the people who are responsible for it are letting you down. *I* could be letting you down."

Devon shook his head, disgusted with himself.

"There are a lot of folks who would skin me alive if they knew that," he continued. "A lot of folks who taught me better than that. I guess maybe I've been away from here so long I've forgotten a few things."

But whether it was being back in Dunbar that made him remember what he'd been taught growing up, the values that had been instilled in him, or whether it was just holding the baby as he was, something clicked for Devon, and in that instant, he knew what he had to do. He knew that there was only one thing he *could* do.

"If you're mine, I'll make this right for you," he vowed to Harley. "I don't really know how, but I will."

It would be an awesome responsibility and the full weight of that settled over him. But he meant what he'd said. If this tiny human being belonged to him, he would make sure Harley was taken care of. That he had everything he needed.

The bedroom door opened again, and Ethan stuck his head in. "How're we doing in here?" he asked, obviously working to suppress his amusement.

"Everything's under control," Devon answered as if it was, when, in fact, everything felt pretty out of control, as if he'd just hooked himself on to a runaway train.

But that was his problem to deal with, not Ethan's. Not Harley's.

"So you're doing all right?" Ethan asked.

"Hey, if you can do it, I can do it," Devon countered with a bravado his brother would recognize.

But deep down he only hoped that it was true that he could do what Ethan had done with Hannah, what Aiden had done with Mickey.

What he'd just promised Harley he would do.

That he could rise to the occasion and be Harley's dad.

If that's what he was.

"You've been awfully quiet since we left Dunbar."

Keely was so lost in her own thoughts that she barely heard Devon's comment.

It was just after one o'clock on Sunday afternoon. They'd had a lovely brunch with his brothers, sisters-in-law, and all three babies, and when Aiden and Emmy had left for Denver to catch their plane for Brazil, Keely and Devon had headed for Ryland to find Brian Rooney.

"It seems as though I should be the one dreading

this meeting, and here you are instead, all with-
drawn," Devon added.

"I'm not dreading meeting Brian Rooney," Keely
finally answered.

"Did I do something that rubbed you wrong?"

The thought of him rubbing her at all was appealing enough to titillate her and bring her slightly out
of the doldrums she was in. Even if notions like that
were the last thing she should be entertaining.

"No," she assured him. "You didn't do anything
that rubbed me wrong."

"You hate this sweater, then," he joked as if he
were a fashion-obsessed teenage girl. "It makes me
look fat."

Keely laughed at that. He had on blue jeans and a
navy-blue turtleneck sweater that hugged every inch
of his broad shoulders and impressive pectorals and
accentuated the denim-blue of his eyes. If anything,
he looked rugged and suave at once. And even more
eye-poppingly handsome than usual.

"Nothing could make you look fat," she said as if
he'd been serious.

"Then it's your outfit. You put it on and decided
later that you don't like it," he guessed. "Well,
you're wrong. Those jeans fit you so well that I had
to step on Aiden's foot to get him to stop staring at
you from behind—and him a just-married man,"
Devon lied flagrantly. "And on top—" he kissed the
tips of his fingers and released the buss into the air
like an Italian chef "—perfection."

On top was nothing more than a charcoal-gray

scoop-neck T-shirt and his mock rapture over it made her laugh yet again. "You're crazy," she decreed.

They were in his SUV, driving through the flat plains of eastern Colorado. There wasn't another car on the country road that led to Ryland. It gave him the freedom to take his eyes off his driving long enough to reach across the gearshift and squeeze her forearm in one big, warm hand.

"Come on, what's bothering you?" he urged, without any teasing in his tone now.

She tried not to notice how good his hand felt on her arm, or the skitter of sparks that ran from that spot all the way through her. But it wasn't easy. It wasn't easy even when he took his hand away. And answering his question seemed like just about the only thing that might act as a diversion. So she opted for doing that.

"Harley is what's bothering me," she said. "Leaving him."

"Want me to turn around? We can go get him and bring him with us."

"No, I don't think it's a good idea to have him there when I do this. Besides, what's bothering me is more complicated than that."

"It isn't only that you're worried about leaving him with strangers? Not that you should be. Ethan has had that nanny checked out thoroughly. Plus, he and Paris will be there."

"No, it isn't that."

"Then what is it?" Devon asked patiently.

"It's how I felt leaving him."

"Were you glad to get away?"

Keely laughed again. This time wryly. "No, I wasn't glad to get away. The opposite, in fact. It was hard leaving him."

"And it shouldn't be?" Devon said, sounding confused.

"No, it shouldn't be. It means I'm getting too attached."

Devon nodded. "Yeah, he kind of has a way of getting to you, doesn't he?"

That comment surprised Keely, and she turned her head to look more closely at her oh-so-striking chauffeur. "You?"

Devon shrugged his acknowledgement, as if he was a little embarrassed to admit outright that he had some feelings of his own when it came to Harley.

"Well, that's good for you—and for Harley—if you end up being his father. But it's not good for me no matter what. In fact, it's very, very bad for me."

Devon glanced at her again, smiling, "*That* bad?" he asked as if nothing could be *that* bad.

"Yes, *that* bad. He's not mine."

"Well, no, he isn't," Devon said rationally. "But if it makes any difference to you, I'd say you're the best thing that's happened to him in his short life."

"Still…"

"Still, if you're getting attached it will be harder to lose him," Devon surmised.

"Yes."

"Okay…" he said, drawing the word out as confusion echoed in his voice again. "But why does this sound like a much bigger deal to you than I would expect?''

Keely debated about whether or not to answer that. To tell him about the biggest regret of her life, and why it was having an impact on her now.

But in the end she decided there wasn't any reason not to tell him. That in fact, he might as well know that she was unavailable for a rerun should Harley be his son and should he have any ideas about her continuing to take care of the baby for him the way she had since before they'd met.

''I was married,'' she said then, skipping any segue.

''Okay...''

''I was married to a man who was much older than me. A widower. With a thirteen-year-old daughter, Mary.''

''Really,'' Devon said, his interest obviously piqued.

''Alby Kent. He owns—''

''Kent Luggage. I travel a lot, remember? I'm pretty familiar with suitcases.'' Devon glanced at her again. ''So you were married to Alby Kent?''

''I was,'' Keely answered fatalistically.

''How did you meet him?''

''He hired me, actually. Just after my grandmother passed away. He had a brother he hadn't seen in years—they'd had a falling-out—and he wanted to see him again, patch things up.''

''Did you find the brother?''

''I did.''

"And the romance started from there?"

"Mmm," Keely agreed dubiously. "At any rate we began to date from there."

"But it wasn't romantic?"

"Actually, now that I think about it, no, it wasn't very romantic. Just dinners out, mostly. But Alby was an interesting man and I fell in love with him anyway—in spite of the age difference and not much effort to sweep me off my feet."

"And then you got married," Devon said, to help the story progress.

"And then we got married."

"And his daughter was the kid from hell," he said, making it sound like the teaser for a horror movie.

Keely laughed, appreciating his attempt to lighten what was a difficult story for her to tell. "No, Mary was not the kid from hell. She was thirteen, introverted, and sadly in need of attention."

"And you provided that?"

"That was really the reason he wanted me," Keely answered.

"No!" Devon said with disbelief.

"Oh, yes. I had no idea when I married Alby that what he was actually looking for was someone to be Mary's mother. His late wife had apparently done the job alone before her death, while Alby tended to business and was essentially an absentee father. When his first wife died and he was the only parent Mary was left with, he wasn't about to fill the void himself. He'd tried nannies and governesses, but Mary was becoming more and more introverted. Depressed, even. And he'd decided that if she missed her mother, he should just get her another one.''

"So he married a new mom for his daughter,'' Devon concluded.

"Exactly. Not that I realized it. For five years Mary and I were a family and Alby... Well, Alby was sort of a drop-in dad and husband.''

"In other words, neither you nor his daughter saw much of him after the wedding.''

"He kept saying that eventually he'd take some time off or solve whatever problem needed solving, and then he'd be around more. But it never happened. There was always another problem to solve or a new outlet to open or a new distributor to woo or...something. There was always something. But I had Mary and I guess that made it a little easier to accept. Although I also wanted to have kids of my own and he never found time for that, either. And then, after five years, Mary turned eighteen, graduated from high school and went off to college.''

"That sounds pretty ominous,'' Devon observed.

"I was still hanging on to Alby's promises and with Mary gone and a lot of time on my hands, I wanted a baby.''

"But Kent didn't.''

"He definitely didn't. I should have seen it coming. I mean, he was no kind of father to Mary, why would he have wanted more kids? But—''

"You loved him and gave him the benefit of the doubt.''

"Blinded by love,'' Keely joked. But neither of

them laughed. Then she continued. "He said he finally had Mary off his back, there was no way he was getting into that again with another child. I sort of saw the writing on the wall at that point and realized he didn't really want me, either. That he'd only married me to replace his wife in Mary's life. And when I said that, he admitted it was true. That he was never going to be the kind of husband I wanted, that he was not having any more kids, and that maybe I should think about moving on to find those things."

"Nice."

"Mmm."

"So basically you were just phased out."

"I'd done my job and become obsolete," she confirmed.

"And that was it for the marriage?"

"The divorce was final four months after Mary left."

"So what about Mary? Did you get some kind of visitation privileges?" Devon asked.

"She was eighteen," Keely reminded. "Our seeing each other has been up to us since then."

"And do you see each other?"

Keely didn't answer that quickly, feeling all the mixed emotions she always felt about Mary.

But after a moment she said, "We see each other periodically. But she's busy and an ex-stepmother is not high on the list of priorities."

"So you *were* close, and now the daughter has phased you out, too."

"It isn't something I *blame* Mary for. It's the same

for anyone starting off on her own. She's busy. She has a lot of friends. A lot of activities. And Alby is her father—if she's going to see a parent, she of course has to see him first. Plus, it's sort of awkward. I loved her like my own daughter but she *wasn't* my own daughter. She was my stepdaughter. And now that she isn't even that, it's… I don't know, it's strange. And painful. I see her, I see this person I thought of as my child, this person I raised basically on my own for five years, and now everything is different. I'm not a part of her life. She's not a part of mine. We're more like old acquaintances and things are…superficial, I guess.''

"Not to mention that she also has to be a huge reminder that you were used by her father for his own purposes.''

"That, too,'' Keely agreed, admitting what she'd never even told her sister.

"And that's why it bothers you to think you might be getting too attached to Harley. Who also isn't yours,'' Devon concluded.

"I swore after the divorce that I would never let myself get involved with someone else's child. Never. That I'd never take on raising someone else's child. Because in the end, that's who they belong to—someone else. And all the love and affection and time and struggles I invested, everything I gave of myself, just bought me a whole lot of heartache. A *whole* lot,'' she repeated, feeling awash in that heartache merely from the telling of this tale and from thinking about

Mary, the person she would forever consider her lost daughter.

"So feeling attached to Harley is like a warning sign, is that it?" Devon asked.

"A great big, glaring warning sign."

They'd reached Ryland by then and were in the center of a town smaller than Dunbar. Devon turned onto a residential street and found the address they were looking for painted on a yellow and white clapboard, single-story house.

He parked at the curb in front of it.

But before putting an end to what they'd been talking about, he angled toward her and said, "Is there any comfort in thinking that you helped fill a void for this girl who'd lost her mother and had a jerk for a father?"

"Sure. It's not as if I regret my time with Mary. I loved her as much as I loved her father and, frankly, I had more fun with her than I ever did with him. Plus she turned out to be a really terrific person and I like to think some of that came from my influence. I'm proud of that. But life moves on, and, under these circumstances, her life has moved on without me being any part of it. Without me having any hope of ever being a part of it in the future."

Devon nodded his understanding and the warmth in his blue eyes helped ease the unpleasant feelings washing through her.

But they were in front of Brian Rooney's house and they could hardly sit there and dwell on things long gone by, on things Keely didn't want to dwell on anymore. So she said, "But that's all in the past and we're here to deal with what's happening in the present."

"In other words, let's get this show on the road?" Devon asked with a hint of a smile.

"Right."

But now it was one of the low points in Devon's history that was facing them and he didn't seem too eager to rush it.

Rather than getting out of the SUV his gaze went beyond her to the yellow house and he studied it as if he could see through the walls. And didn't particularly like what he saw.

"You're sure this is the place?" he asked, sounding as though he hoped she might be wrong.

"This was Brian Rooney's address as of a week ago. So, unless he's moved since then, this is it."

Devon nodded. But he stayed put.

"You don't have to do this, you know," Keely said then, attributing his reluctance to second thoughts. "You could just wait for me out here."

"No," he answered. "I want to make sure what needs to be done is done. For my sake and for Harley's."

Something about the way he said that, coupled with his earlier comment about Harley having got to him, gave Keely a strong sense that something had changed in Devon's feelings toward the baby. But now was hardly the time to investigate it.

"I'll make sure what needs to be done gets done,"

she assured him instead. "You don't have to be in on this."

His eyes returned to her, more earnestly even than before. "I don't want you to do it alone, either," he reminded her.

He finally got out of the SUV and came around to open her door, too.

"Let's just get it over with," he said as she joined him on the sidewalk.

But getting it over with was easier said than done because when they rang the doorbell there was no answer.

There was also no answer to their knock or to their second and third rings.

And when Devon went to the side of the house to peer into the window in the garage door, he reported that there was no car inside.

They'd come too far and seeing Brian Rooney was too important just to give up. So they opted for going across the street to the park to wait where they could watch for him.

Which was how they spent the remainder of the day and into the evening before the need for food sent them to the restaurant they'd had plans to go to.

But Brian Rooney still wasn't home when they returned, nor did he show up, and by eleven that night their patience was exhausted.

"You don't think he's gone on vacation or something, do you?" Keely asked.

"Anything's possible. He could have just spent the weekend with a girlfriend and he'll be back tomorrow. But one way or another, it's too late now to ask around.''

"Which leaves us where?" Keely asked.

"Headed for Dunbar to sleep and make this drive again tomorrow, or spending the night in that little motel we passed earlier," Devon said.

"Are you just trying to get me to a motel?" Keely asked, joking.

"You found me out. The truth is, I slipped out of Ethan's house while you were sleeping last night, came to Ryland where I tied Brian up and stashed his car, then drove back to Dunbar so I could come here today and lure you to the Triple Bar S Lodge for some down-and-dirty debauchery.''

"Oooh, my favorite kind," Keely answered his joke with her own, making him laugh.

"So, do we stay or do we go?"

"It seems more practical to stay," she decided.

"Then it's the Triple Bar S for us. One room or two?" he asked with mock hopefulness.

"Two rooms," she said.

"Damn. I'm just having no luck at all today," he said with that wicked grin that could send shivers up her spine all by itself.

The Triple Bar S Lodge was made up of six white stucco cottages that formed their own cul-de-sac behind the office and living quarters of Ed, the owner and manager. Each cottage held two side-by-side rooms—each with its own bathroom—so Keely and Devon had one entire cottage to themselves.

It was nearly midnight by the time they had checked into the motel and called Ethan to let him know they wouldn't be back tonight. After a long day and evening together Keely thought she should be tired of Devon's company. But as it was, when he suggested he come by her room so they could share the cheesecake they'd bought at the restaurant to eat on the drive back to Dunbar, she was still glad for just a little while longer with him.

So, by twelve-fifteen Devon had made a stop in his own room and was knocking on the door to hers, causing her pulse to race all over again, as if this were the first time she'd seen him today.

She was, however, surprised to find him not only with the single-slice cheesecake box in hand, but with an overnight bag.

"The tools for the down-and-dirty debauchery?" she asked with a nod at the bag as she let him in.

"I never leave home without them," he said with a wiggle of his eyebrows. Then he set the cheesecake and the satchel on the coffee table and explained. "I keep an emergency bag in the tire compartment of the SUV. I've been out shooting film once or twice and decided on the spur of the moment to stay over someplace, so I've learned to be prepared."

He opened the bag and dug around inside for a moment before bringing out an extra-large white T-shirt he offered her to sleep in, two toothbrushes still sealed in their original packaging, two tubes of toothpaste—one nearly used up and the other new—

and a travel-size stick of deodorant. Women's deodorant.

"Okay, even if I don't ask why you have two toothbrushes, I can't be left in the dark about the ladies' deodorant," Keely said.

"Clarissa," he answered simply enough. "The last time I packed the bag she would have been likely to head into the wilderness with me, so I put in a few things for her, too. The occasion never arose, though, so the stuff hasn't been used."

"As long as you don't just drive around with women's deodorant in case you pick up someone of the female persuasion," Keely said, accepting his offerings.

Then Devon produced two plastic forks along with two bottles of water he'd purchased from the vending machine beside the main office, and they sat on the sofa—angled nearly face-to-face—to eat the cheesecake that Devon held for easy access.

"So," Keely said then, giving in to another wave of curiosity. "Hasn't there been anyone since Clarissa to use your emergency supplies?"

Devon's expression sobered so much it made Keely wonder what she'd said wrong. "Sore subject?" she asked when she saw it.

"More of a sore subject than Clarissa," he admitted.

"I wouldn't have thought that was possible."

"What Clarissa…and Brian…did, hurt me. And I turned around and hurt someone else. That makes it a sorer subject."

More surprise. "Did you go out and hurt someone on purpose?" Keely asked.

"No, not on purpose," Devon answered with a humorless chuckle at the very notion. "But even accidentally it's still something I wish I hadn't done. Something I feel badly about."

"What did you do?"

They'd polished off the cheesecake and Devon set the empty container on the coffee table before he sat back again and stretched an arm along the top of the cushion behind Keely.

"I had a rebound relationship with a woman named Patty Hanson," he said then.

"Did *you* cheat on *her?*" Keely guessed.

Devon's brow furrowed into deep grooves. "How would I cheat on someone accidentally?" he asked. But before she had the chance to answer, he said, "No, I would never do that. To anyone. But what I did do was get involved with Patty because she was the exact opposite of Clarissa, and I thought that was a good thing."

"It turned out not to be?"

He shook his head. "We wanted different things. She was…wholesome. Homespun. She'd never so much as traveled out of the state and she didn't have any desire to. She wanted marriage, a family, a house with a white picket fence, a husband who always stayed as close to home as she did."

"Which wasn't you."

"No," Devon agreed. "It wasn't—isn't—me."

"That's how you hurt her?" Keely asked, confused.

"I hurt her," Devon explained, "because I guess in some way I must have led her to think that *is* what I am. Or maybe that that's what I could be in time. I don't know. I never thought I was misleading her. I was upfront about what had happened with Clarissa and how glad I was that Patty *wasn't* another wild woman…that she had morals and values…that she wasn't an irresponsible, self-centered fly-by-night. But in the end, to her, that somehow seemed to mean that I would be all the things she wanted in a man, too. That I was ready to cash in my plane ticket—permanently—and just take up residence on the recliner beside her in front of the television."

Keely had to smile at the absurdity of anyone believing Devon would fit into that scenario.

"Anyway," he continued, "when she told me that was what she had in mind for me, I let her know there was no way. That we didn't have the same vision of the future."

"And that hurt her?" Keely asked.

"Oh, yeah," he confirmed. "She completely flipped out. She kept saying she could whip me into shape. That all I had to do was try to be what she wanted and we'd both be happy—"

"Wait, wait, wait, wait," Keely said to halt his rush through what was obviously a deep guilt he carried. "If I'm hearing this right, you were glad—after Clarissa—to have the kind of woman this Patty was, but she wanted you to be something different than what you are. And when she figured out that you weren't what she was looking for, she wanted you to change so you would be.''

Devon let that sink in and then he said, ''I never thought about it like that. Patty was so upset with me, so hurt, she saw it as my failing her and so did I.''

''Well, stop it,'' Keely ordered. ''It doesn't sound to me like *you* misled *her*—and believe me, after Alby Kent's assurances that he wanted a strong family life, that he wanted everything I did, that it was just a matter of time before that's what we had together, I'm experienced in being misled. But if you didn't misrepresent yourself that way, it sounds to me like this woman misled herself.''

''That's a lot nicer interpretation from my perspective,'' he said without sounding as if he truly felt absolved of his guilt.

But his expression did relax again as he grinned at her and used the hand that was resting on the back of the couch to smooth her cheek in a featherlight stroke. ''All I know is that Clarissa left me leery of party girls and Patty left me afraid of you wholesome, girl-next-door types.''

''I fit in that last category, do I?'' Keely asked, not sure she liked it.

''You seem to. You're definitely not like Clarissa.''

Which sounded like a good thing so Keely tried not to take it too seriously that he'd said he was also afraid of that category of woman he'd put her into.

''So you're scared of me, huh?'' she asked even as

he lit tiny fires in her blood with that gentle caress on her face.

''Terrified,'' he said in the sexiest voice she'd ever heard and with a half grin that made it seem as if he were joking.

He slid his hand down the side of her neck, then to her nape, then to her shoulder so his arm was around her to ease her nearer. Near enough for his mouth to take hers in a teasing, playful kiss.

On its own, her hand went to the thick, strong column of his neck, learning the texture. The tautness of the tendons tensed as he turned his head to deepen the kiss.

And just like that all those little fires he'd lit in her veins flared into bigger ones.

His other hand came to the side of her waist, closing around it to pull her closer still, almost onto his lap. Her breasts just brushed his chest, but it was enough to turn her nipples into tiny pebbles in response.

His lips parted over hers and the kiss deepened, intensifying as his tongue made a call on hers, toying with it like a cat with a mouse and turning her on even more.

Not that Keely didn't give as good as she got. Because she did. Her own tongue played its role in every game. Danced every dance he instigated. Answered every query with a boldness born from the heat of those infernos licking at her from the inside out. Those fires fueled by Devon, by the scent of his aftershave, by the taste of him, by the nearness of him, by feeling his arm around her, his hands on her.

That hand at her waist coursed down her outer thigh then, stopping at her knee to squeeze it before he retraced the path, traveling higher than her waist now, going all the way to the scant side of her breast as their mouths clung together. Kissing. Coming up for air. Kissing again, only with mouths open even wider. Mouths that grew hungrier and hungrier. Savoring the mingling of their breath. The hot velvet of combined lips, the thrust of tongues that mimicked other, more intimate things.

Keely's whole body seemed ablaze by then. Ablaze with a craving, with a need for him.

She let her hands slide under his sweater to just the base of his bare back, then she inched them up the widening V, rolling over mounds of muscles to his shoulders, reveling in the silken feel of his naked flesh.

He seemed to take it as encouragement because he found the hem of her T-shirt and slipped both of his hands under it, pressing his palms to her back.

His touch felt so wonderful she writhed with the pure pleasure of it. Or maybe with the yearning for even more. For the feel of those hands on her engorged breasts that strained against him.

He must have felt it, too. Or at least wanted the same thing she wanted, because he made quick work of unfastening her bra and then those long-fingered hands found her breasts, enclosing them in his warm grasp, kneading, teasing, learning just how to drive her completely wild. So wild her head fell away from his kiss as a moan escaped her throat.

Never had she wanted anything—or anyone—as much as she wanted Devon at that moment. Devon, who was more excruciatingly handsome than any man she'd ever known. Devon, who was more exciting. Devon, who could make her heart pound with just a glance. Devon who could wipe away all thought, all reason, and leave only pure, unadulterated desire. Devon, who…

Who was the one man she should *not* have been losing herself with.

It was only a little voice in the back of her head that reminded her of that. Yet it was a powerful little voice. Delivering a powerful reminder.

Oh, how she wished that wasn't the case! Not when he made her feel the way she felt at that moment.

But no matter how she felt, the little voice had made its point and she knew she had to stop this before it went any further.

"No more," she heard herself nearly groan.

"No?" he asked as if she were kidding. "No more of this?"

He kissed her again so passionately she almost wilted.

"No more of this?" he said, circling her nipples with his thumbs until they were so tight with craving that they almost ached.

"No more of anything?" he said, flexing the long, hard ridge of his desire for her against her hip to let her know what else he had in store for her.

A part of her shrieked that yes, she did want more! More of everything he'd just done. More of what she only imagined he could do from there. More of him.

But now that that other part of her had remembered that this man could put her into the same kind of mess that had hurt her so badly in the past, she couldn't overlook it.

And that was the part that won.

"No more of anything," she said firmly enough to let him know she genuinely meant it this time.

Devon drew in a breath so deep it was almost a gasp, but he stopped. He took his hands away. He gave her one final, chaste kiss, and then leaned back against the arm of the sofa as if only distance could keep him from going on.

Then he closed his eyes for a moment, as if to get some control over himself before he opened them again and gave her a half smile. "This must be how motels get their reputations. Maybe it's something that comes through the ventilation system and goes right to your head."

Keely was grateful that he was taking this so well. "Maybe," she agreed, playing along. "Or it could have been the cheesecake."

"Cheesecake as an aphrodisiac? You might be right."

Keely was also grateful that he didn't ask why she'd stopped him. Grateful that he was making light of the whole thing.

He closed his eyes a second time, and she had the

sense that it was for the same reason as the first. This time, when he opened them once more, he also stood.

"Well, whatever it was, I'd better get out of here before it kicks in again."

"Probably not a bad idea," Keely said. Especially since just looking at him made her rethink her decision and consider asking him to move with her to that bed that was so nearby.

"Shall we try to hit Brian's place again early in the morning?" Devon asked.

Keely had some trouble switching gears enough to register what he was saying, but she struggled out of her own fantasy to recall their real purpose for being in Ryland, in that motel.

"We probably should," she agreed. "To catch him before he goes to work or if he just runs by his house for a change of clothes or…whatever."

"So when shall we check out? Seven?"

"Okay."

"Seven it is, then," Devon said, looking for all the world as if he might dive back onto that couch again with the slightest provocation—or invitation.

But Keely was too tempted to do just that—to invite him back. And she knew she had to resist it. So she stood, too, to walk him to the door, crossing her arms over her chest to hold her unfastened bra in place as Devon took his cue to go.

He grabbed his just-in-case bag from the end of the coffee table and headed for the door, saving her from herself.

"I'll knock at seven," he told her on the way.

"Good."

"And in the meantime, if you need me—" he cut himself off, letting her know he'd meant that innocently enough, only it had come out sounding insinuating. "Well, you know," he said with a slight chuckle before he left.

Never had any room seemed as empty as that one did once he'd gone.

But she'd done the right thing, Keely told herself.

It was just that it didn't feel that way.

Not when every fiber of her being was crying out for him. For his arms to be around her. For his mouth to be ravaging hers. For the touch of his hands. For everything he could be there doing to her.

If only she wasn't so worried about what might be at the end of this road.

Chapter Eight

Keely and Devon were parked in front of Brian Rooney's house when he arrived home at about nine the next morning.

He was tall—at least six feet—lean, and slightly lanky. He had dirty-blond hair that was in need of a trim, unremarkable hazel eyes and a full beard. He was an attractive man, but Keely thought he was pale in comparison to Devon.

When Brian Rooney realized it was Devon getting out from behind the steering wheel of the SUV his face lit up like a kid's at Christmas.

''Dev!'' he said with so much undisguised hope in his voice that Keely felt a little embarrassed to see it.

Devon, on the other hand, responded with nothing more than a courteous, ''Brian.''

Then he introduced Keely and let Brian Rooney know that it was Keely who had come looking for him.

"I need to talk to you, Mr. Rooney," she told him.

"Brian," he corrected, to let her know she needn't refer to him so formally. But his expression was suddenly confused.

Keely knew his first thought had been that Devon had come to see him and that she was merely the tagalong rather than the other way around. So as soon as he'd let them into his house, she wasted no time explaining why she was there so he wouldn't get his hopes up that Devon had come to reconcile with him.

The moment she finished telling him about Clarissa and Harley and that he might be the baby's father, he turned his disturbed frown to Devon again and said, "This is why you're here? You didn't come for any other reason? Just about some kid?"

"Clarissa named him Harley," Devon said without hostility, but as if he hadn't appreciated hearing Harley referred to as "some kid."

And it occurred to Keely that anyone hearing only Devon's portion of this would never guess that the two men had ever met before, let alone been friends.

Brian Rooney ignored the information about the little boy who might be his son and instead repeated his previous questions. "And that's it? That's all there is to you being here? It's just so we can go have some blood test to see which of us is stuck with Clarissa's bastard?"

Keely flinched at that and saw a muscle tense in

Devon's jaw. For a time that ugly word hung in the air. Then, in a voice that was obviously tightly controlled, Devon said, "I don't ever want to hear you call him that again."

"That's what he is, isn't he?" Rooney said. "After all, she wasn't married—to either one of us. What else do you call the product of a slut like that?"

"Never again," Devon warned, not addressing the rest of what Rooney had said.

"Never again," the suddenly extremely angry man mimicked. "Right. Got it. Yes, sir. Anything you say, sir."

Keely wondered if he was trying to provoke something. If allowing Devon to be in on this had been a mistake not because of Devon, but because of the other man.

Although, even if Rooney was trying to start a fight, Devon wasn't taking the bait, and, after another moment, Rooney seemed to relapse into that initial hope he'd greeted Devon with.

"I've told you how damn sorry I am for what happened with that…with Clarissa," Rooney said. "I'd do anything to put it behind us."

"It is behind us," Devon answered evenly.

"But you won't forgive it. You won't let things go back to the way they were before," Rooney said like a pouty child.

"They can't go back to the way they were before," Devon said reasonably.

"They could. If you'd let them."

"No, they couldn't, Brian. The water under that bridge is just too murky. All we can do now is move on."

"Move on like we don't have any history together? Like we weren't practically brothers? Just because I messed up?"

Messed up? Rooney said that as if he'd done nothing more than lose Devon's baseball glove.

"We've gone over all this before," Devon said. "I'm not here to rehash it. I'm only here because one of us is Harley's father and we need to sort out who."

"Why?" Rooney demanded, furious again. "I don't care if it is mine, I don't want anything to do with something that came from *her.* I don't want to see it. I don't want to know it even exists. I don't care what happens to it."

At that point it was Keely who wanted to hit Brian Rooney.

She didn't, of course. But over and above appearance, the more she heard from this man the more she had to wonder what Clarissa had seen in him, how she could possibly have cheated on Devon with him.

She did, however, decide that it was time for her to step in and get back to business. So, working to keep her own emotions from echoing in her voice, she said, "We need to determine who Harley belongs to. After that, if he's yours, that doesn't mean you have to take him. You can relinquish custody the same way Clarissa did and I'll make other arrangements for him."

Brian Rooney looked from her to Devon, as if it were really sinking in that nothing between them was on the verge of repair. His temper flared hotter still. "Forget it. You do the test," he said to Devon. "If he's yours, he's yours. If he's not, do with him whatever you want."

"That's not how it's going to work," Devon answered calmly but with a note in his voice that quietly intimidated. "I've had the blood test and now so will you."

"Oh, right. So somebody can hit me up for child support forever?"

"No, so this baby can be taken care of the way he needs to be," Devon said matter-of-factly.

"He's probably not mine," Rooney said, showing the first signs of backing down.

"We can all hope that's true," Devon said, surprising Keely. "But one way or another, we're going to find out."

After having Brian Rooney's blood drawn at the local doctor's office, Keely and Devon took the sample with them and returned to Dunbar to pick up Harley before continuing on to Denver.

Devon wasn't very talkative and Keely left him to his thoughts. She knew the encounter with Brian Rooney couldn't have been easy for him.

Certainly it hadn't been easy for her. It had left her with grave concerns about how this situation was going to turn out for Harley if Brian Rooney proved to be his father.

She had hopes that Devon would do the right thing if he was Harley's dad. After all, Devon had already made some effort to become acquainted with the baby. He'd also shown concern and provided the things Harley needed.

But Keely didn't have to get to know Brian Rooney to see that he was unable to separate Harley from the woman Rooney now apparently hated and blamed for irrevocably ruining his relationship with his best friend. It had clearly caused the kind of resentment that didn't go away, the kind of resentment that meant that Harley would never have a home with him.

If Brian Rooney had fathered Harley, Keely knew she was going to have to put the baby into the system to be adopted. And the thought of that broke her heart even more than the idea of turning him over to either man.

It was barely three o'clock that afternoon when Keely, Devon and Harley got back to Denver. A still-quiet Devon took Keely and Harley to Keely's house and, after carrying the baby and bags inside for her, he left for a late meeting.

Hillary was home working, so once Keely had Harley down for his nap she took the blood sample to the lab and ran some neglected errands.

By the time she got back, Hillary and Brad were cooking dinner together, and Harley was in his carrier nearby, watching. Keely set the table while she filled them in on the events of the weekend.

Most of the events of the weekend, anyway.

She omitted her encounter with Devon after

the wedding and the fact that they'd very nearly made love.

She also didn't tell them that something, somewhere along the way, had changed for her. That something had changed in her feelings for Devon. And in her feelings for Harley, too. Something that had her thinking that the results of that blood test to determine who Harley's father was could impact her even more than she'd ever considered.

Worrying kept her preoccupied during their meal and all through putting Harley to bed that night. She just kept thinking that by the next day there would likely be an answer about who Harley belonged to. The answer would either get Devon off the hook as Harley's dad and leave him no reason to have anything else to do with either Harley or with her, or it would place Harley in Devon's hands and leave her with the need to save herself from the same kind of situation she'd been in with Alby Kent by never seeing Devon...or Harley...again.

Whichever scenario played out tomorrow, her connection to Devon, her reasons for having contact with him, were about to come to a conclusion.

Not that she had any doubts that that was for the best. She knew it was. But even knowing that didn't keep her from feeling that, by sitting at home with her sister and Brad the remainder of the evening, she was wasting what precious little time she had left. And the last excuse she had to be with Devon.

It didn't escape her that that wasn't altogether rational. Of course, it made more sense to stay away from him when every minute she was with him seemed to get her in even deeper. And since the end was in sight, what she should actually be doing was distancing herself from him. Cutting her losses.

But the outcome of the blood test was weighing on her, and Hillary and Brad were cuddling right under her nose and making her feel particularly lonely and envious of what they shared. And it all made her want to be with Devon even more. She wanted the distraction of him, the comfort he seemed to provide. She wanted this one last evening with him, in spite of what tomorrow would bring, in spite of the fact that she knew the more time she spent with him the harder the parting would be. In spite of everything.

This was her last chance, she kept thinking. Her very last chance.

Regardless of how sorry she might be later on that she hadn't distanced herself when she'd had the perfect opportunity to, regardless of how sorry she might be that she hadn't cut her losses, in the end it didn't matter. In the end, she just couldn't deny herself spending one more evening with him.

There were lamps lit in Devon's living room when Keely parked her car at the curb in front of his house. But there was no sign of him through the undraped picture window.

She turned off her engine, but she didn't get out of the sedan. Instead she sat there watching the house, knowing this was not the wisest decision she'd ever made.

Knowing that didn't make her restart the car and leave, though. Instead, when she saw Devon come through the door from the kitchen into the living room, she took her keys out of the ignition.

For another moment she just stayed where she was, watching him as he sat on the couch that faced the window and did something with the camera she'd seen him use the day at the zoo. He checked lenses and looked through his camera bag.

He was dressed in a pair of jeans and a plain white T-shirt that hugged his torso like a second skin. And that simple sight of him was enough to make her ultra-aware of the surface of her own skin, of the sudden tiny knots her nipples became. It was enough to make her forget why she'd ever thought she shouldn't come here in the first place, and to wonder what she was doing out here watching him when she could be inside *with* him.

So she opened the car door and got out.

From inside the house Devon must have sensed someone was there because he came to the picture window, peering through the glass with a curious expression on his strikingly handsome face. Then, realizing it was her, his expression erupted into a smile, and he disappeared through the archway that connected to the entry, opening the front door just as she climbed the steps to the porch.

"This is a nice surprise," he said with a note of question in his voice. "Don't tell me you have lab results already."

"No, the lab said it would take until tomorrow."

She didn't hesitate to enter the warmth of his foyer when he stepped aside in silent invitation, adding as she did, "I just wanted to make sure you were all right after today. You were pretty quiet on the drive home."

Okay, so she was grasping at straws to explain showing up on his doorstep. But she couldn't very well have told him she was there because she couldn't make herself stay away from him.

"I was just aggravated with Brian and I didn't want to lay it on you. But I'm cooled off now," Devon informed her, closing the door.

"Maybe I shouldn't have bothered you then," she said, afraid her excuse wasn't strong enough to get her by after all.

"As a matter of fact," he confided, leaning close to her ear, "I was just wondering if I could spring another visit on you like I did after the bachelor party."

So if she'd waited he would have come to her. That made this seem less awkward.

"How about a glass of wine?" he suggested then. "I think we've earned it today."

Keely agreed, and Devon escorted her into the living room and seated her on the sofa before he went into the kitchen.

While he was gone Keely caught sight of herself reflected in the glass of the picture window. She had purposely not changed her clothes when she'd finally given in to the urge to come here because it had been important to her that this not seem like anything more than a casual, friendly drop-by to see if he was suffering any ill-effects from his encounter with his former best friend.

But now she wished she had at least put on something more flattering than the oversize striped shirt and the faded jeans she always wore for comfort.

She'd taken her hair out of the ponytail it had been in and brushed it. And refreshed her blush and mascara. But still she suddenly longed for clothes that didn't look as if she'd borrowed them from a brother.

"Nectar of the gods," Devon announced when he returned a few minutes later with two glasses of a rosy liquid.

He handed one to Keely and joined her on the couch, facing her and propping an elbow on the sofa back.

"Here's to a happy ending for this whole thing," he toasted, clinking his glass to hers.

"I'll drink to that," Keely said as they each took a sip of wine.

Once they had, Devon leveled those penetrating blue eyes on her and said, "You were pretty quiet yourself after we left Brian."

"I suppose I was."

"Did he upset you or was it something I did or said?"

"It wasn't you," Keely assured.

"Then it was Brian," Devon concluded. "I know the things he said about Harley ticked me off. Is that what got to you?"

"They definitely weren't heartening."

Keely took a sip of wine and then hazarded a question that had been on her mind all day. "Did you mean it when you said you hoped Brian Rooney wasn't Harley's father?"

"Oh, yeah," he answered without hesitation and with enough emphasis to let her know he honestly did mean it.

"But if Harley doesn't belong to Rooney, he belongs to you," she pointed out, testing.

Devon didn't respond to that as readily. There was a moment's hesitation before he said, "I won't lie to you. If Harley is mine it's going to shake things up pretty big for me."

"That's true."

"But I made up my mind Sunday that I'll do what I have to do. *Whatever* I have to do."

"Meaning you'll do whatever you have to do to raise him? Or to find him other parents?" she asked for clarification.

"I'll do whatever I have to do to raise him."

Even though she was hoping that would be his answer, it still surprised her slightly.

"What made you come to that decision on Sunday?" she asked.

Devon shrugged. "Ethan brought Harley in to me early that morning to take care of for a while."

"And you realized you can?"

Devon laughed. "Actually, I was really bad at it. I was just hoping he'd go to sleep or something. But he wouldn't. He wanted a bottle and I had to give it to him. But in the process we came to a meeting of the minds,'' Devon finished as if he were letting her in on a great mystery.

Keely played along. ''Ah. A meeting of the minds,'' she responded with mock solemnity.

But then Devon's tone lost the levity. ''The thing is, even though I tried not to, I ended up having to hold him. And when I did…'' Devon raised his free hand, fingers splayed. ''He's just so damn little,'' he finished as if something about that hand in comparison to the size of Harley had been a turning point for him. ''Anyway, it just hit me that he's helpless. Defenseless. And if I'm responsible for his being here…well, then it's up to me to make sure he's taken care of. So, if he's mine, I'll deal with it.''

Clearly, it still wasn't an idea he was comfortable with, but Keely thought it was a step in the right direction.

''And if Harley is Brian's,'' Devon continued before she could say anything, ''then you and I are going to have to make damn sure we get him to people who will give him a good home and a great life.''

That surprised her, too. Keely had expected that if Harley proved to be Brian Rooney's son, Devon would simply breathe a sigh of relief and wash his hands of the whole matter. Yet here he was, wanting to take some responsibility for the infant one way or another. The man just never failed to amaze her. Or impress her.

''It matters to you what happens to Harley even if he isn't yours?'' she asked.

"Yeah, it does," he said as if he was slightly shocked to discover that himself.

Keely just shook her head as she looked at that handsome face, at those incredible blue eyes, at the cumulative magnificence of him, thinking that even though it was all pretty spectacular on the outside, there was still so much more to him than the packaging.

"You're really something, do you know that?" she heard herself say before she realized she was going to.

He grinned. "Well, yeah," he joked as if it were about time that occurred to her. But his tone lacked all arrogance and she knew he *was* only kidding.

He combed his fingers through her hair then, cupping the back of her head gently as his eyes held hers.

And in that moment she saw a bad-boy sparkle come into them that warned her he had other things on his mind now. Things she probably shouldn't have opened the door to.

But she had. She'd opened the door by coming here. And now that she had, she couldn't make herself close it again.

He pulled her slowly closer. Slowly, slowly closer, keeping his gaze trained on hers all the while. And when she got close enough, he kissed her. Fiercely, right from the start. Deeply. Passionately. As passionately as he'd left off kissing her the night before in the motel.

And heaven help her, she was kissing him back every bit as fervently. As hungrily. Knowing deep down that this was the real reason she'd come here tonight.

But Devon couldn't have known that, too, and so he cooled things down after only a moment, easing into a kiss that was almost chaste. Almost tentative. Until he stopped altogether so he could look into her eyes again.

He brought that one big hand from the back of her head to the side of her face, caressing her cheek while he seemed to search for a sign that this was what she wanted.

And even though there should have been signs galore that it *was* what she wanted, what she'd been yearning for since the moment she'd stopped him the previous evening, he must not have trusted what he saw because he said, "Is tonight different than last night?"

Keely let her head fall forward, resting her brow against his chest as she thought about that.

Tonight *was* different. It was her last chance not only to see him, to be with him, it was also her last chance for this, too. To have satisfied the driving needs he'd brought to life in her. To go away with the knowledge of what it was to belong to him completely, what it was for him to belong completely to her even for only a short while. To at least have the memory to take with her.

"Yes, tonight's different," she answered him in a breathy voice. "But don't ask me to explain why."

He didn't. He took her at her word and merely

tipped her chin upward again with a single index finger so he could recapture her mouth with his.

But this kiss was short-lived, too, because Devon stopped it to stand and take her hand, pulling her with him to turn off all the lights and then to abandon the living room, to take her upstairs.

There could be no question then about what they were going to do, and on that walk she gave herself one final option to end this before it went any further.

But if she didn't go through with it, she knew she'd regret it. That she'd forever be left wondering what it would have been like.

So, rather than turning tail and running, she whispered, "I didn't bring anything. Protection, I mean."

"Leave it to me," Devon said as he reached the door to his bedroom and stood aside for her to go in ahead of him.

Like the rest of the house, it was strictly a male domain. Plain. Simple. Serviceable. Masculine. And made up primarily of a bed that was so big it went nearly wall to wall.

But the room was clean, and the bed was made and covered in a brown quilt, and when Keely stepped inside she could smell the faint lingering scent of Devon's aftershave wafting from the adjoining bathroom, familiar and welcoming and enticing all at once.

He kissed her again in the room lit only by the light from the hallway, filling his hands with her hair, kissing her with more of that urgency that had begun this.

His mouth was open and so was hers as she snaked

her hands under his T-shirt to indulge in the satin-over-steel feel of his naked back.

Devon wasted no time unfastening the buttons of that oversize shirt she wore, letting it dangle as he unsnapped her jeans and pushed them down. Her shoes and socks came away with them and she was left in her shirt and her lacy bra and matching thong.

He divested himself of his own T-shirt and opened the snap and zipper of his jeans just enough to let her know he didn't have anything on underneath them.

He returned to kissing her, maneuvering them both onto the bed on their knees where he ran his palms from low on the outer sides of her thighs, to her rear end—cupping it for a moment in both hands to pull her tight against him before he continued up her back, under her shirt to her shoulders, her sides, and finally around to breasts that hadn't stopped aching with the need to feel his touch since the last time.

The man had incredible, big, adept hands. Talented hands that knew just how firm a grip to use. Just how much pressure. Just how much tenderness. Just what to do to arouse and tease and torment while his mouth still ravaged hers, while his tongue plundered and everything together wiped away thoughts of all but what he was doing to her, what he was reawakening within her.

He slid her shirt off, and rather than feeling self-conscious Keely just wanted the bra and panties to go, too. To be rid of everything that was still between them.

Once the shirt was gone apparently Devon had the

same thought because he unhooked her bra and rolled her thong away, too.

And then she had those hands on her without any barriers at all. Those palms enclosing nipples that hardened so quickly it was as though that was where they were meant to be.

His mouth abandoned hers to kiss her chin, the column of her throat, trailing the tip of his tongue along the hollow and over to her collarbone, to her shoulder where he began a leisurely descent that made her writhe with the anticipation of things to come.

He pressed her to lie back, coming with her, partially on top of her so those kisses could reach her breast when his hand gave it over. His hand then sluiced down her arm to entwine his fingers with hers, raising her hand above her head and bringing her breast more fully into the hot wetness of his mouth.

Sucking. Nipping. Tugging. Amazing her with sensations that all made her blood run like lava to other spots that were beginning to cry out for him.

He lowered her hand then, in an arch along the mattress, pulling it forward and placing it on the outside of his half-lowered jean zipper.

Keely was only too happy to explore the solid ridge of him there. To let the zipper open the rest of the way so she could reach behind it, to enclose him in her hand and drive him as crazy as he was driving her.

His hand did more traveling then. Finding his way between her legs to take her another step toward insanity.

He slipped a finger inside her and her spine arched all on its own, bringing her off the bed with the pure pleasure of it.

"Does that mean you don't hate that?" he asked with a chuckle as he drew that finger out and forward, and then back in, making her gasp.

"No, I don't hate that," she barely managed.

"How about this?" he questioned as he plunged in even deeper while it was his thumb he sent sliding forward this time.

She was incapable of answering him then. She could only stay frozen in the throes of that delight that very nearly pushed her over the edge.

"Oh, no, not yet," he said in a ragged voice, taking his hand away to replace it with something even better, quickly sheathing that part of him before introducing it to her, letting her become accustomed to the size, the heat, before he inched into her farther. And farther still, filling her with that long, hard staff that felt so good she couldn't help tightening around him.

He kissed her again. Or at least what passed for kissing with mouths wide and tongues dueling. His body moved into hers as she arched to accept him, pulled as he drew out and arched again when he returned. It was perfect rhythm. A metered dance that grew faster and faster until the pace became frantic. Until each thrust was like riding an ocean wave.

Keely hung on to Devon's strong, broad back as he plunged so deeply into her that their bodies melded into one, carrying her into the crest of that wave, into the ultimate peak of pleasure that robbed her of breath and made him groan as pure, potent ecstasy washed through them at the same time.

And then the wave began to ebb. By degrees. Subsiding. Easing them gently back to shore.

Keely finally drew a breath that came replete with a high-pitched moan.

Devon relaxed, muscle by muscle.

His breathing was heavy and warm in the tangle of her hair. His skin was slightly damp and so was hers. And it wasn't easy to tell where she left off and he began.

"Are you okay?" he asked in a ragged voice.

"I'm good," she managed in a bare whisper.

Devon left her then, lying on his side and urging her onto hers so he could press his front to her back, molding them together. Then he pulled the quilt over them for warmth and wrapped his arms around her to keep her close against him as exhaustion settled over them both.

And in the cocoon of quilt and man, she couldn't fight her own fatigue.

But as she drifted nearer and nearer toward sleep, she wasn't the least sorry she'd come to him tonight, that she'd seized this last chance, that they'd made love.

Because there was one thing she knew for certain.

No matter what the next day might bring, this had all been worth it.

Chapter Nine

Keely was still sound asleep when Devon woke up at eight the next morning. She was lying on her side facing him, snuggled into his body.

With a single index finger he very carefully moved a long strand of curly red hair away from her face so he could have an unobstructed view. Then he lay very still and studied her, drinking in the sight of that thick, wild mass of hair haloing her fine, delicate features; of her long eyelashes resting against her high cheekbones; of her flawless skin and perfectly shaped lips parted only slightly as soft, even breaths passed through them.

She really was beautiful, and it was as if simply looking at her fed something inside him. Simply looking at her made him feel content. Complete. Just plain happy.

It also made him want to do what he'd done twice more after they'd made love the first time. He wanted to wake her up with kisses and make love to her again.

He just couldn't seem to get his fill of her. Of course how could he when making love with her was so damn incredible? When it was the most incredible lovemaking he'd ever had?

But four times in less than twelve hours? He should probably give her a break.

Or at least a little sustenance before the fourth time.

He couldn't resist pressing a light kiss to her forehead. Or indulging in the sweet scent of her hair. And the truth was, he thought he could have stayed in that bed with her forever, whether they were making love or not.

Still, a fourth round was an appealing idea and with building her strength in mind, he secured the sheet, blanket and quilt around her to keep her warm and slipped out of bed.

Keely sighed slightly in her sleep. A soft sound that made him smile. Made him want to climb back in with her and pull her into his arms all over again. He managed to resist that urge. Breakfast, he reminded himself. He was going to fix her breakfast, maybe draw her a bath.

Maybe take the bath with her…

He snatched the jeans he'd worn the previous evening from the floor and put them on, silently leaving the room and hoping Keely stayed asleep so he could have the pleasure of waking her again when he got back with food. Then he padded down the stairs.

About the time he reached the entryway he heard a funny, melodious ringing from somewhere in the living room.

He wasn't sure what it was and made a detour to investigate.

It took him a moment to figure out where the ringing was coming from, but it kept up and he finally realized it was Keely's cell phone.

The tiny phone was sticking up out of the top of her purse and he wondered if there was some kind of etiquette about this that he wasn't aware of. Should he take it up to her? Should he answer it himself? Should he just let her voice mail take a message?

Taking it up to her could very well ruin his plans, so he discarded that idea. Which left him debating about answering it or leaving it to voice mail.

But then he thought, what if there was something wrong with Harley and Hillary was trying to reach Keely? And that sent him to at least check out the display to see if there was any indication of who the caller was or if there was an emergency.

So he picked up the phone.

The display told him who the caller was all right. But it wasn't Keely's sister. It read Lab and had a number underneath it.

The lab. It had to be the lab she'd taken the blood samples to. Maybe with the test results that would let him know if he was Harley's father.

Thoughts of etiquette disappeared and, acting

purely on nervous impulse, Devon answered the phone.

"This is Susan from Denver Independent Laboratories calling for Keely Gilhooley," the voice on the other end of the line said in response to Devon's hello. "May I speak with her, please?"

"She's unavailable right now," Devon informed the woman. "But if you're calling with the results of the blood test to determine paternity of Harley Coburn, I'm one of the people involved so you can tell me."

That didn't go over well. The lab technician wasn't willing to divulge the information to anyone but Keely so it took some work and giving the caller his name, his address, his telephone number and his social security number, to convince her that she was revealing the confidential information to one of the people entitled to have it.

But he finally succeeded in persuading her, and then he waited with his heart in his throat as she recited blood types.

"For Clarissa Coburn we have A positive. Brian Rooney is A negative. B positive for Devon Tarlington. And B positive for Harley Coburn—"

"Harley and I have the same blood type," Devon said, interrupting the woman before she dragged this out any longer.

"Yes, sir."

"Am I assuming correctly that since Harley's blood type is different from both his mother's and

Brian Rooney's, that Brian Rooney couldn't be his father?''

"Yes, sir."

A simple enough answer that the person on the other end of the line didn't realize had enough of an effect on Devon to deflate him onto the couch as if he'd just had the wind knocked out of him.

He didn't really hear anything else the lab technician said after that before he hung up.

He just kept thinking that Harley was his.

He was a father.

A father...

Harley was *his*...

He'd thought he was prepared for this, but it still hit him hard.

There was no question about it. Harley was his kid. His son.

"Oh, man..." he said out loud.

He felt numb. Numb and maybe a little relieved that Harley didn't belong to Brian Rooney.

That was a good thing, he reminded himself. He hadn't wanted Harley to be Brian's after the man had let it be known how he felt about Clarissa and about Harley because he'd come from Clarissa. So it was good that Brian *wasn't* Harley's dad.

"But I am," he said under his breath.

And now he had to do what he'd said he would. He had to *be* Harley's dad.

His mouth was suddenly very dry. His heart was pounding pretty hard, and that panicked feeling he'd felt when Ethan had left him alone with Harley Sunday morning replaced the numbness.

But he was determined not to give in to the urge to run the other way. Clarissa had already abandoned this baby and there was no way he was going to.

So. Okay. He was Harley's father.

He could handle this, he told himself like a coach firing up his team before a big game. If Ethan could handle it, if Aiden could handle it, he could handle it.

Thinking about his brothers helped. They were both doing the whole parenthood thing and doing it well, as far as Devon could tell. And there was nothing they could do that he couldn't.

Except that he'd always lived a more nomadic lifestyle minus a lot of ties or commitments or attention to the home front.

"I'm just going to have to get domesticated," he said, trying it on for size.

Actually, he was surprised to find that the fit wasn't too bad.

After all, when he thought about it, he began to believe the domestication wouldn't be *too* much different from what he'd been doing since Keely had first knocked on his door with this news. And that had been okay. In fact, it had been fun taking her and Harley to the zoo with him. It hadn't even been so bad shopping for baby gear or having dinner with Keely and his family with all the babies in tow. And even getting Harley to bed every night hadn't been horrible. Especially when afterwards he'd spent the rest of the evenings alone with Keely.

Of course, it did occur to him that Keely was a recurring theme in all that. That she'd done the work. That she'd made it seem easy. That her company, her sense of humor, her outlook, her personality had made it pleasant and enjoyable.

But this wasn't a package deal, he reminded himself. Harley was his. But Keely wasn't.

That thought threw him into a second tailspin. An even worse tailspin than learning that Harley really was his.

Not only wasn't Keely included with Harley, she'd only been around *because* of Harley and *until* she resolved who Harley's father was. After that, she could very well plan to say goodbye to Harley *and* to Devon…

The panic Devon had chased away returned double force at the possibility that he could be gaining Harley and losing Keely, and his immediate inclination was to do absolutely anything he had to do to keep that from happening.

"Wait a minute. Think about this," he advised himself when the direction his thoughts were headed became obvious to him, and when flashes of Patty Hanson also began running through his brain like little warning signs.

Being with Patty in his post-Clarissa funk had been like curling up in a flannel blanket with the stomach flu. It had been just what he needed at the time. It had felt good. Warm. Comfortable. Comforting. That was where the real interest, the real appeal had been.

But when he hadn't needed that comfort anymore, his interest in her and her appeal for him had waned in the same way his desire to hunker down with a blanket evaporated when he recovered from the flu.

So, was that an element now? Was part of Keely's appeal as a safety net? Or was he wanting Keely for Keely?

He hadn't been hurting when he'd met Keely, he reasoned. He hadn't needed comforting, so that wasn't a factor with her. And she'd appealed to him anyway. Big-time. So the fact that she appealed to him now seemed to be separate from everything else going on. It seemed to be *in spite* of it all, actually.

But there were similarities between the two women and Devon knew he had to take that into consideration for the long haul. The last thing he ever wanted to do was hurt another woman the way he'd hurt Patty by not being able to meet her expectations, by disappointing her, by letting her down. He couldn't face another woman who ultimately might not have enough spice to maintain his interest.

Although just thinking about that in comparison to Keely made him smile at the pure absurdity of it. Keely, bland? Not hardly. Yes, she was a home-baked-bread kind of woman on the surface. She was responsible. Down-to-earth. Practical. All the things Patty had been. All the things Clarissa *hadn't* been. But underneath, Keely had plenty of spice. In her sense of humor. In her spirit. In the bedroom…

It was simply a more subtle brand of spice. Something that came out strongest when they were alone— whether in the bedroom or out of it. But that was something he'd discovered he liked better than Clarissa's public displays. It was nice that he alone got the benefit of it with Keely. It left him feeling more confident in her loyalty.

So really, he thought, Keely was a combination of Patty and Clarissa. A combination of the best parts of them both.

And, Devon recalled, hadn't that been what Aiden had said at the bachelor party? That Keely didn't seem like Patty or like Clarissa, that Keely just seemed like herself?

At the time the idea hadn't had much impact on him, but it did now.

Keely was like and unlike Clarissa. Keely was like and unlike Patty. Keely was Keely and that was exactly the way he wanted her.

And brother, did he want her! So much so that it occurred to him that even the thought of domestication—as long as it was with her—had an allure all its own.

Devon laughed a wry little laugh at himself.

Was that the key? he wondered. Was that how it happened? Settling down, doing the family thing, became conceivable when it was with the right woman?

It certainly seemed possible, since just weeks ago he would have sworn he was a long, long way from ending up with a wife and kids, and yet here he was, feeling pretty good about exactly that.

But the more he thought about it, the more he knew that Keely *was* the right woman for him. The entire image of his future, of raising Harley, of domestication, had a kind of rosy glow to it with Keely in the picture.

So, sitting there in his living room, with Keely upstairs asleep in his bed, all of a sudden everything became very, very clear to Devon. He was Harley's dad and Harley should have the stable foundation that the people of Dunbar had given the Tarlington boys. The roots, the grounding, the knowledge that he was wanted and cared for and loved. All those things that Devon believed had given him the courage, the self-esteem, to go out into the world, to travel, to be the man he was. Harley deserved that, too, and he needed to provide it for him. He *wanted* to provide it for him.

And he wanted to do it all with Keely by his side. Keely, who would round it out. Who would be his partner. Who would make it fun. Who would make it perfect.

It struck Devon then that he couldn't wait for her to know all this. To know that Harley was his and that he wanted Harley to be hers, too. That he wanted the three of them to have what they'd had in this time since Clarissa had put them together.

So he dropped her cell phone back into her purse, stood, and went into the entryway where he bounded up the stairs, hoping the entire time that *he* was what *she* wanted.

* * *

Keely wasn't too sure what had initially drawn her out of her dreams, but the sound of Devon's voice coming from downstairs had brought her fully awake even though she couldn't make out what he was saying.

At first she thought he had company and she debated about whether to stay in bed—essentially hiding—or dress and go down, pretending she'd just come up here to the bathroom.

Then the talking stopped and in the ensuing silence she wondered if he had just been on the telephone.

If that was the case, she thought, he might come back to bed. So she rolled to her back and waited.

As she did, her mind wandered to all the lovemaking that had taken place in that bed in the past few hours. To how much she would like to have Devon make love to her just once more before she had to leave.

But he never came back. And after a while she decided she didn't want to be lounging in his bed while he went about his business—if that's what he was doing down there. So she opted for getting up.

She dressed in the clothes that had been so hurriedly discarded the night before and then went into the bathroom to wash her face and run her fingers through her hair.

She'd never been as glad to have her wild curls. Because of them her hair rarely looked too tame so even a mere finger-combing took away the just-out-of-bed look. She did wish she had some mascara and blush, but even without it she judged herself not too much the worse for wear and headed out of the bathroom.

When she opened the door, Devon was standing in the middle of the bedroom waiting for her.

"Oh. Hi," she said a bit tentatively.

He gave her the once-over, ending with his eyes meeting hers and a lazy smile stretching a mouth she now knew was incredibly agile.

Then he said, "I was hoping to come up here and find you still in bed."

He only had on jeans and the waistband button was undone, exposing a dark line from his navel downward, disappearing behind his zipper and making her think too much about what else was behind it. Then, too, his exquisitely cut bare chest and shoulders and his bulging biceps didn't help keep her mind on getting home to Harley and Hillary, either. Even the morning shadow of the beard that made him look scruffy was so sexy Keely could barely see straight.

She tried hard, though. "I heard your voice coming from downstairs," she said to his comment that he'd been hoping to find her in bed, knowing it wasn't really an answer, but coming up with the best she could when her brain and body were busy wanting a fourth replay of the previous night's events.

Apparently the comment worked as a segue for Devon because he said, "I answered your cell phone—that must have been what you heard. It was ringing and the display said it was the lab."

That made her pause.

"Already?" she said, dreading the news that would change everything.

"Already. The results of the blood tests were in."

He didn't seem unhappy about it, but Keely didn't know what that meant. "And?" she prompted.

"Harley is mine."

Devon hadn't hesitated to admit that. There wasn't any reluctance at all. But still she wasn't sure congratulations were in order, so she said, "How do you feel about that?"

"I'm okay with it. I'm actually glad he didn't turn out to be Brian's."

"I'm glad of that, too," she said, although it wasn't forceful. Not that she'd wanted Harley to belong to someone who so openly despised him. She absolutely hadn't. It was just that now she knew what she had to do and it wasn't easy to accept.

"So, I've been downstairs doing some thinking," Devon said then, interrupting her thoughts.

"I imagine you have."

"About you."

"About me?" she said, confused. "What about me?"

"About you and Harley and me. And how things have been since you showed up at my door. And how I want things to be from here on."

The hairs on the back of Keely's neck stood up. She was very, very afraid of what he was going to say next.

"I was thinking that I want you to be a permanent

part of this little family I unwittingly started,'' he told her.

What Keely wanted was to cry. Just that quickly tears welled up inside her. But she didn't. She merely shook her head. ''I won't be your bailout,'' she said in a quiet voice that echoed with remorse.

Apparently that was the last thing he'd anticipated hearing because his eyebrows shot up and he reared back slightly. ''Bailout?'' he repeated. ''Who said anything about you being my bailout?''

''That's what I'd be, wouldn't I? The person who takes care of Harley, who raises him, while you go about your business?''

''No, that's not what I had in mind.''

''Isn't it? That's what you've done this last week,'' Keely pointed out.

''This last week I didn't know whether or not he was mine. But now that I do, things will be different.''

''That's true,'' Keely agreed. ''Things will be different. And I know it won't be easy for you and you'll probably need some help. But I can't be the person who gives you that help, the person you use to make it easier.''

''The person I *use?*'' he said, frowning now. Those big, glorious hands she'd reveled in so much the past night were on either side of his waist as one insolent, angry hip took most of his weight. ''Is that what you think?'' he demanded. ''That I want to *use* you?''

''Maybe not intentionally, but—''

''Not in any way at all. I want you to be a part of

the future here. Of my future. Of Harley's. I was hoping that might be what you would want, too.''

"I do want it," she admitted. "But I can't have it.''

"Why not?" he demanded. "You said that's what your goals for yourself were—a husband, kids. And that's what I'm offering.''

Keely laughed without any humor at all. "That's the point. You're *offering* it—like a job.''

"Damn it, Keely, that's not true.''

"Really? Because that's what it sounds like. I'm just guessing, but have you decided to change occupations and do some kind of photography that keeps you at home, or did you think you could go on traveling as much as you always have because I'd be here with Harley? Have you decided to dive in and be a hands-on dad or did you decide that the last week wasn't so bad and if you could have me around the whole time things could go on like that?''

"The only thing I *decided* was that I want you to be a part of everything that happens around here from now on.''

That sounded good, despite the touch of anger in his tone. And it was more tempting than he probably realized. So tempting that had Keely not had the experiences she'd had, she would have jumped at the idea.

But as it was, she was just too worried about the part he wanted her to play in his and Harley's future. Too worried to simply hope for the best and plunge in the way she'd done with Alby Kent.

No, regardless of how she felt about Devon, about Harley, she had to abide by the decision she'd made when her head was clear and uninfluenced by her heart. The decision she'd made before she'd met Devon. The decision never to be the surrogate parent to someone else's child while that someone else took the opportunity to go on with his life so he didn't have to fulfill his responsibilities.

"What do you want then?" Devon asked. "Do you want to be a hands-off part of things? Because if that's what it takes to get you to say yes, then I'm telling you right now that I'll make sure you never lift a finger."

"You know that's not realistic. And it's not something I could ever do. Which is the point. If I'm around, I'm going to be who takes care of Harley and you won't put the effort into it that you need to. And you do need to put effort into it, Devon, or you'll never really be Harley's father. I know you can do it. I've seen you come to care for him, to care that he has what he needs, to care about what's best for him, so I know I don't have to worry about his welfare with you. But I also know that it won't be you who really does raise him unless I step aside and give you the opportunity."

It was his turn to shake his head. "You're wrong, Keely. I'm going to be hands-on whether you're here or not. All you'd have to do if you feel like I'm not carrying my share of the load is tell me."

"Right. And you'll make promises to do more as soon as your next trip to New Zealand or the Arctic

Circle or Timbuktu is over. But it won't happen,'' she said sadly.

"Why won't it? Because it didn't happen with your ex-husband? Are you forgetting that I'm not Alby Kent?''

"No, I'm not forgetting who you are. You're a man who's found himself suddenly, unexpectedly, unwillingly, a father, and it isn't something you want to face alone. It isn't something you feel capable of handling on your own. So I'm the quick fix. Handy. Available. Already familiar with your son.''

"You are so damn much more than that,'' he said very slowly, enunciating each word.

"I'd like to think that,'' she said softly. "But I just can't.''

"So what are you going to do? Just walk out of here, have Harley delivered to me and never look back?'' he said as if he didn't for a minute believe it.

"That sounds like a plan,'' she confirmed much more flippantly than she felt.

"And last night? What was that? Your final fling?''

She couldn't answer that. Not only because she didn't want to admit it was true, but because her control over those tears that had been threatening was suddenly very tenuous and she knew she had to get out of there before she lost it completely.

So all she said was, "I'll have Hillary work the rest of this out with you.''

Then she headed for the bedroom door to go.

But she had to pass by Devon as she did and

one of those big hands shot out to grab her arm to stop her.

He leaned over enough so that his breath brushed her ear. "Don't do this," he nearly whispered. "Give us a chance. You can always get out later if I don't make you happy."

But Keely knew from experience just how painful that eventuality could be. And she just couldn't run the risk of ever having to go through it again.

"No," she barely managed.

And then she pulled herself from the warmth of his hand on her arm and left.

Chapter Ten

Hillary's wedding the following Saturday was a quiet, elegant affair with a relatively small group of friends and family.

Keely was her only attendant and as she stood beside her sister during the ceremony she tried hard to hide the fact that she was really only going through the motions, that she couldn't concentrate on the vows, that, even though she was happy for her sister, she just couldn't find pleasure in the event.

But then why should today be any different? she thought. After all, she hadn't enjoyed a single thing since walking out of Devon Tarlington's house the day after they'd made love.

It was ironic, really. She'd refused to be a part of Devon's and Harley's lives to protect herself from ever again feeling as awful as she had when Mary Kent had gone off to college and Alby had let her know her services as wife and mother were no longer needed. Yet there she was, feeling awful just the same.

After the ceremony at the small chapel not far from their house, the reception was held at an event hall nearby. Not even champagne helped Keely's spirits and she merely mimicked someone having a good time while all the while she was really counting the hours until the whole thing was over.

Hillary and Brad stayed right to the end, only retiring to the dressing rooms to change into more casual clothes to leave for their honeymoon after the last guest had departed.

The plan was for Keely to take the wedding gown home for her, so, as Hillary carefully removed the white lace dress, Keely busied herself with the hanger and plastic covering that was to go over it.

"You won't forget to take this to the cleaners on 48th so they can do whatever it is they do to keep it from yellowing, will you?" Hillary said as she handed it over to Keely.

"I won't forget," Keely assured her sister, thinking more about going home to their empty house than about that. Thinking about spending the next full week alone there. She had work to do, but that wasn't going to keep her distracted every minute of every day—and night—and even with distractions it was difficult not to think about Devon and Harley. Not to wonder what they were doing, how they were faring, if they missed her as much as she missed them.

A knock on the dressing-room door preceded Brad saying, "I'm ready when you are, Hill."

"I'll be right out," Hillary called back, putting on her coat. Then, as if she knew what Keely was thinking, she said, "Are you going to be all right?"

"Sure," Keely answered, too enthusiastically.

But her sister saw through it. "I think you should just pay them a visit," she said out of the blue.

"Who?" Keely played dumb.

"You know who. Devon and Harley—the two people you've been beating yourself up over since you made me take Harley to Devon."

"I haven't been beating myself up over them."

"Keely, you've been crying all week and that smile you've plastered on for today isn't hiding anything. Iris Nelson asked me if you were having back problems because she said you were so stiff, you looked as if you were in pain."

"Iris Nelson isn't playing with a full deck, we've always known that."

"But this time she's right." Hillary remained staring at Keely. "Come on," she urged. "Just go see how they're doing. Go see if Devon is acclimating to fatherhood. Maybe he'll surprise you."

"And so what if he does surprise me and he is acclimated to fatherhood?"

"Then maybe you can rethink your position. Maybe he's turned into Super Dad and proved he isn't like Alby at all and here you are, not even knowing it when you could possibly be working this out with him.''

"Brad is waiting for you," Keely reminded her rather than addressing that.

It didn't matter. Hillary continued anyway. "Look, I know this is a touchy situation because you've already gotten burned once before. But you must really care for this guy if you're this down over *not* being with him. And I know you spent more time with Harley than I did and got more attached. So now that that's all happened...well, maybe you just need to give it a shot."

"Or not," Keely said.

"Come on, Keely, I'm worried about you."

"Don't be. I'm fine."

"You are sooo not fine," Hillary insisted. "Just go over to Devon Tarlington's house and see him and Harley. Think of it as a follow-up. As something you owe to Harley. To make sure he's okay, that he's being taken care of."

"Social Services assured me they would assign Harley a caseworker and keep an eye on things."

"Go yourself anyway. Tonight. It's only five-thirty and you're ten minutes away. Go! Go! Go!" Hillary said as if she were frustrated with Keely and it had just come to a boil.

"No, *you* go—on your honeymoon—and don't give me a second thought."

Hillary stared at her a while longer, as if that might wear Keely down. But Keely was stubborn and she just out-waited her sister until finally Hillary gave up.

"Suit yourself. Be miserable for maybe no good reason."

"I'm fine," Keely repeated, ushering Hillary out to meet her groom.

And then Keely was alone. And definitely not fine. In fact, she was miserable.

She put on her coat, catching sight of herself in the mirror as she did. She looked slightly ridiculous in a knee-length trench coat over the hunter-green, slinky, formfitting floor-length bridesmaid gown. But what difference did it make? She was only going home to her empty house.

She gathered up her sister's wedding dress and left the hall, too, without saying anything to the cleaning crew already busy at work.

It was cold in her car, the precursor of the winter storm predicted to hit before morning. Some reports were saying that it could be an early blizzard that could paralyze the city and the thought of being snowed in didn't cheer her up any.

Then, as she turned the key in the ignition, another thought occurred to her.

What if the storm really was that big, and Devon hadn't planned ahead and stocked up on diapers and formula for Harley?

That seemed like a possibility. After all, he was new to parenthood and the first storm of the winter could catch people off guard. So maybe she *should* swing by his house after all, just to mention to him that he should be prepared.

''Oh, you're pathetic,'' she said to herself as she pulled out of the hall's parking lot.

Hillary had planted the idea of seeing Devon and Harley and now here she was trying to find an excuse to actually do it.

Well, she wasn't going to. Surely Devon knew enough to have an ample supply of whatever he needed, and what he *didn't* need was her popping in to tell him.

Even if popping in might allow her a little peace of mind.

But it would allow her only a very little peace of mind, she knew. Because while she might end up with it on one front, she also knew that seeing the two of them would stir a whole lot of other things she'd been working hard to control.

It was just a bad, bad, bad idea, and that was all there was to it.

So what was she doing at the stop sign at the end of Devon's street? Where all she had to do was make a left turn and go down two blocks to his place?

''Don't do it,'' she warned as if she were talking to someone else.

But when the time came to make the turn, she did it anyway, feeling powerless, a moth drawn to a flame.

She was disgusted with herself, and she knew this was a really stupid thing to do. She knew she was no better than a hormonal teenager with a crush on someone, driving by that someone's house.

But she *was* only going to drive by, she told herself.

And she meant it, too.

Except that somehow when his house came into view the car seemed to slow down all by itself. And park at the curb.

"What did you make me do, Hillary?" she moaned.

But she stayed right where she was, staring up at the red-brick abode.

Even though it was barely six in the evening, it was dark enough for there to be lights on in Devon's living room so she could see into it through the picture window, just as she had the last time she'd come here. Devon was nowhere in sight and she knew she could have driven off without him ever knowing she was there.

But she couldn't make herself do that.

Not that she got out of the car, because she didn't. She merely sat there, frozen by her own indecision.

Then, just as on the last occasion, Devon came into the living room from the kitchen.

Only this time he was carrying Harley. On his hip.

And every thought instantly drained from Keely's mind as she devoured that view framed by the picture window.

She watched as Devon went to his stereo, marveling at how comfortable he seemed with Harley now. It was already as if he were an old hand, not even thinking about what he was doing carting the baby around at the same time he slid a CD into the stereo's tray.

They both looked good. Devon had on tight jeans and a gray mock-neck T-shirt. Harley was dressed in a red-and-white-striped turtleneck and a pair of denim overalls, contentedly sucking the index and second fingers of one hand, apparently as comfortable with Devon as Devon was with him.

She should have been thrilled to see it. They looked as if they were both doing well. As if they'd become accustomed to each other. And that was good. That was great.

It was just that it somehow made Keely feel so left out.

Inside the house Devon went about his business, pressing a big hand to Harley's small back to spin around as if he'd been carried away by the music he'd apparently just turned on.

Harley's fingers came out of his mouth and he seemed to be laughing as Devon began to dance a fast two-step that delighted them both.

It was sweet and funny and touching all at once, and it made Keely laugh a little even as it ached not to be in there with them, not to be sharing that bit of spontaneous fun.

So why, when she could clearly see that Devon and Harley were okay, was she sitting there making herself feel even worse by watching what she couldn't be included in?

It was crazy.

As crazy as coming here in the first place.

As crazy as it was to suddenly find herself getting out of the car and heading for the house.

What am I doing?

She didn't know. But she did it just the same, going all the way up onto the porch and ringing the doorbell.

The music stopped.

Mere moments passed while Keely told herself to run back to her car and drive away.

And then the door opened and there they were.

Devon and Harley.

''Is it party time already—'' Devon said before he realized who she was.

Then he stopped short. His eyebrows arched toward his hairline and his voice went from welcoming to shocked.

''Keely!''

The problem with being at the mercy of impulse rather than rational thought was that she didn't have a plan or any prepared excuse for her appearance on his doorstep. So, with nothing to say, for a moment she just stood there, staring at the big man holding the small baby, able to think only that she must look like an idiot standing there in a bridesmaid's dress and a trench coat.

Then she managed a simple ''Hi,'' wondering as she did who else he'd been expecting when he'd opened the door. If it had been another woman. A date, maybe.

Devon recovered from his surprise then and said, ''Come in.''

She could hardly refuse. Although she almost did because now that she'd done this she was afraid it was a mistake. A big, huge, hairy mistake.

Still, she stepped into the warmth of his entryway and remained staring at the stairs while he closed the door behind her.

Turn around and say something! she ordered herself.

But even when she did turn around, the vision of Devon, of Harley, close up, wrenched her insides so severely she still couldn't think of anything to say.

"I don't know what I'm doing here," she whispered then, hating that she sounded so forlorn.

"I don't care what the reason is, I'm just glad you are."

That helped. It helped a whole lot.

"Come on," he said. "Get out of that coat and come into the living room and sit down."

Keely obeyed, with Devon following behind.

Off went the trench coat and she sat at one end of the sofa much as she had that very first day when she'd been on a mission to tell him he might be a father. Although, as unnerving as that had been, at least she hadn't been dressed formally for it.

Devon sat at the other end of the couch, settling Harley on one leg. Harley smiled at her around the fingers that were back in his mouth.

"Hi, angel," Keely said then, heartened to see that he remembered her. "Will you come to me?" she asked, extending her hands to the infant.

Harley leaned forward to give his consent and

Devon didn't resist when Keely reached for the baby, pulling him into her lap.

She hadn't intended to hug him so close, but somehow it happened anyway as she absorbed the feel of having him in her arms again, the feel of him cuddling with her. And Keely had to fight another wave of hot tears at the pure joy of holding the baby.

But once she fought back the swell of wetness in her eyes she finally glanced up at Devon and said, "I guess I just needed to see—"

"Both of us, I hope," Devon said.

Actually, she'd been about to say she just needed to see if everything was all right, but Devon's version was more true. Because looking at that handsome face, being within mere feet of him, was as much a treat for her as holding Harley.

"And you needed to see us so much that you came straight from your sister's wedding," Devon pointed out with a touch of teasing.

"I did come straight from the wedding," she admitted. "Though, to be honest, what I was thinking was of reminding you that—with the storm coming— you should be sure to have enough formula and diapers on hand," she added to keep from seeming desperate.

If Devon knew she was only making an excuse he didn't show it. Instead he said, "Believe me, formula and diapers are not things I'd let myself run out of."

"I couldn't be sure it would occur to you."

He didn't respond to that. He just studied her. And Keely couldn't help thinking that he was waiting for her to get past this small talk to the real point of her visit. But since she wasn't altogether clear what the real point was, she said, "So, are you doing okay?"

He didn't answer immediately. As if he was weighing whether or not to go along with more of this inconsequential chitchat.

But in the end he must have decided to, because he said, "I think we're doing fine. We've pretty much gotten used to each other. He's letting me sleep through the night—for the first two nights he woke up frightened because he didn't know where he was. But now he's staying asleep. I've signed up for a parenting class, if you can believe it. And we've been squeezing by. So far I don't think I've done him any harm and he's being pretty good about my lack of skills. I've even discovered it's kind of nice to have someone to come home to when I've had to be gone and hired a sitter."

And wouldn't she like to be that *someone*.

But Keely chased that notion out of her head and said, "I'm glad."

The doorbell rang again just then.

"That *has* to be Mishka," Devon said more to himself than to Keely.

"Mishka?" Keely repeated the romantic-sounding name curiously. And maybe slightly suspiciously.

"My neighbor. She's always done my housecleaning and shopping and things, and now she's playing baby-sitter and nanny when I need her to," Devon explained as he got up and went to the door.

Wow. He really had accomplished a lot in a short time, Keely thought. A nanny and everything.

A nanny who Keely couldn't help being curious about.

A nanny who Keely couldn't help picturing as young and beautiful and friendly and maybe sexy, too.

But then Devon returned with the nanny in tow. All two hundred fluffy pounds of a woman who had to be nearly sixty. And Keely breathed a silent sigh of relief.

Devon introduced them and then said to Mishka, "I have Harley's diaper bag packed and his coat on the table in the entryway."

It was Mishka who added for Keely's benefit, "I'm taking Harley to my grandson's birthday party."

"She has nine grandchildren," Devon said.

But it wasn't the number of grandchildren the older woman had that was making a dash through Keely's thoughts. It was curiosity about why Devon was having the night off. If maybe he had a date after all.

"Maybe I should go, too. You must have plans."

"No, I don't. Just sit tight," Devon said in no uncertain terms, as if he wasn't about to let her go now that he had her here again.

Mishka said it was nice to meet Keely, and then she and Devon took Harley into the entry.

From where Keely was sitting on the sofa she could see them and she was interested in whether Devon would put on Harley's coat and get him into the car seat or hand the baby over to Mishka to do it all.

But he didn't pass Harley off on the nanny. Instead he did everything, going on to cart Harley and the diaper bag to the nanny's station wagon where he secured the carrier in the back seat himself, too.

It was strange to see him doing all he did with the infant. Strange to see him taking the lead, the responsibility, doing the work when he'd been so standoffish with Harley before. Apparently leaving the two of them on their own had accomplished what Keely had wanted it to and again she knew she should have been pleased by that. But somehow she just felt more of what she had watching Devon dance with the baby— she just felt left out.

It was your choice, she reminded herself.

But even having chosen it didn't change the fact that she wasn't a part of what was going on here.

Then she recalled what Hillary had said when her sister had suggested this in the first place—that if Keely came here and discovered that Devon had turned into Super Dad maybe she could rethink her position. And she began to wonder if maybe she could.

Oh, this could be dangerous.

But she couldn't keep from thinking about it anyway.

She'd denied herself being a part of Devon's and Harley's lives because she'd thought it would end up the way things had with Alby and Mary. But Devon had only been a dad for a short time and already he was handling it better than Alby ever had. Handling it and seeming to enjoy it, if the dancing and the fact that he liked having someone to come home to were any indication.

He actually seemed to be getting into the whole fatherhood thing. He was organized—he'd had Harley and the diaper bag ready when the nanny had arrived. And he was obviously a hands-on dad since he hadn't merely given Harley over to Mishka the moment the woman walked in. He'd taken care of the baby himself. Which was also the opposite of anything Alby would have done.

No, Devon appeared to be embracing his new role.

It surprised Keely but it was true. He'd adapted. He was even going to take parenting classes, for crying out loud. And she had to admit that once again he'd impressed her.

With Harley's car seat strapped into the older woman's back seat, Devon closed the rear door, bent over to say something to Mishka, who was behind the wheel, and then returned to the house.

But when he rejoined Keely he wasn't pussyfooting around anymore.

"So. Have I passed?" he demanded, sitting in the center of the sofa now, much nearer to where Keely was.

"Passed?" she repeated.

"As a dad."

"I didn't come to grade you," she assured.

"Do it anyway."

"I haven't seen anything to find fault with," she told him, meaning it.

"And I suppose that makes you think you were right, that because you left me on my own, I did what I wouldn't have done if you'd stuck around."

"You seem to have proven me right. I thought if I got out of your way you'd do what you needed to do. And it looks as though you have. Or at least you've started to."

"Yep, I'm dad. And mom, too, when you get right down to it. And you were even right about Harley being worth altering things for."

"Things like what?"

"Like my job. I've already set the wheels in motion to cut down on my trips, to focus more on what I can do from here. To use some of the pictures I already have piled up to compile books I've never gotten around to writing. Plus Harley's a good baby. He's easy. As I get better at everything I think I'll be able to take him with me some. Show him the world."

Once more Keely felt left out just thinking about that. But she didn't say it. She just said another, "Good. I'm glad."

"But there was one thing you were wrong about."

"What?"

"I would have done it even if you had stayed." He paused a moment and then he added, "Okay, I admit that forcing me to do everything on my own gave me the whirlwind course in parenthood. And part of the reason I've done what I have in record time was so that I could go to you and try to convince you to come back once you saw that I was completely hands-on. But still—''

''You were going to try to convince me to come back?'' she heard herself ask before she'd realized she was going to.

''That was my plan. Because there's only been one thing really wrong around here since you left, and that's that you haven't been in on all this.''

That was how it felt to her, too. But she didn't want to say it.

And before she could think of another way to respond, Devon said, ''So. Now that you've seen for yourself that I'm a hundred-percent dad, any chance you might want back in? I mean, it seems like I have a chance since we were on your mind so much that you came here right from your sister's wedding.''

There was enough of a hint of teasing to that last part to make her smile slightly. ''I was just going home after the reception and you were on the way,'' she lied.

Devon scooched over closer to her. Close enough so that she could smell his aftershave and the memory it aroused only turned her to mush.

''Come on, Keely,'' Devon prodded. ''Harley and I are having a good time, but we'd have a better one if you were here with us. What would it take?''

Not much.

Although that wasn't entirely true because still she was hesitant to jump in with both feet. It really hadn't been all that long that Devon had been a practicing father. He could still be rooting around more for help with Harley than wanting her for herself.

"I don't know…" she said in answer to his question about what it would take to bring her into his and Harley's life. "I still can't help wondering if we'd be having this conversation if there wasn't Harley."

That made him drop his head into one hand and laugh wryly.

"I can't believe you think that," he said. "That's such a throwback to that other guy."

Then he raised his head again and looked into her eyes. "Think about it," he urged. "Even when I was scared to get near Harley I was still hanging around. Didn't it occur to you that that was because I wanted to be with *you?* I was staying even after you put Harley to bed. I was putting the moves on you right and left. And that last night—what could you possibly think that had to do with Harley? What about any of it left you thinking I wasn't hotter than hell for you?"

Okay, so he had a point. Especially when she compared the way things had been between her and Devon, and the way things had been between her and Alby.

Alby had been attentive to an extent, but right from the get-go the relationship had been more about Keely taking care of Mary than about Keely having much of a romance with Alby.

"No, I can't say Alby Kent ever seemed *hot* for me," she admitted.

Devon inched even closer to her, taking her hand in both of his. "Well I was on fire for you."

"Past tense?" Keely asked.

He grinned a wicked grin. "No, not past tense. If you only knew…" he finished with a groan that made it seem as if abstinence had actually caused him pain.

Then, as his eyes delved deeply into hers, he said, "Here's the thing, Keely. I don't know what brought you here tonight and I don't care because it gives me the chance to tell you what I should have told you that last morning. What I've wanted to tell you ever since. I'm in love with you. I fell in love with you *in spite of* Harley, not because you change a mean diaper. Yes, I think the three of us together would be a great family. But with or without Harley or any other kids, it's you I want."

Keely could feel all her resolve crumbling to reveal only a full heart. A heart full of love for this man. With or without kids…

But still there was one more lesson her past experience had taught her and she said, "What about kids? More kids, I mean."

"We can have a baker's dozen if that's what you want."

"What do *you* want?"

"You," he said simply but forcefully. "You. You. You. A whole life with you. A family with you. To see the world with you. To grow old with you. Everything with you.''

''Oh,'' she said, unable to keep from smiling now.

''So what do you say?''

She let a minute lapse, as if she needed to think about it. But she really didn't. Because suddenly she knew exactly what she wanted.

''I guess I say yes,'' she finally answered. ''To whatever the question is,'' she added when it occurred to her that he hadn't actually asked her anything.

''The question is, will you marry me?''

''Oh. If *that's* the question, then never mind,'' she joked.

But it didn't daunt Devon. He closed what small distance remained between them by wrapping his arms around her and pulling her to him. ''Either marry me or I'll just tie you to the bedposts and keep you as my love slave.''

''You don't have bedposts.''

''I guess you'll just have to marry me then.''

''Well, okay, if that's how it has to be,'' she agreed with a sigh.

''It's about time,'' he said as if she'd made him work hard for that consent.

Then the expression on his handsome face changed. His eyes actually turned a darker shade of blue and the corners of his mouth angled upward with a devilish quirk. ''You know, Mishka won't have Harley back for a couple of hours.''

''No?''

"And I think this deal needs to be sealed."

"With a kiss?"

"For starters."

He did kiss her then. A soft, warm kiss that was just enough to remind her how good he was at it before he got even better. Before his lips parted wide enough for his tongue to greet hers. Before his hands began to course along the surface of her skin as if to relearn the texture, awakening all her nerve endings with the miracle of his touch.

Their kisses became urgent and hungry as she did some relearning of her own, pulling his shirt out of the waistband of his jeans. Sliding her hands underneath to his hard, honed back. Working her way around to his front where male nibs were almost as taut as her own nipples had become.

But then she remembered that undraped picture window through which she'd twice now had a clear view of what went on in the living room and she tore her mouth from Devon's.

"You can see everything from outside," she informed him.

"Who's watching?" he asked in a raspy voice as he nibbled her earlobe and the column of her neck and began to lower the zipper down the back of her dress.

"All I know is that we'd better not do this in plain sight," she said insistently.

But apparently Devon wanted her too badly to waste time going upstairs because he stood, bringing

her to her feet with him so he could toss the cushions
to the floor behind the sofa. Then he took her around
to the back, flung off his shoes and socks, and urged
her down onto the makeshift bed.

''Uh, is this a good idea?'' she asked.

''One of my best,'' he assured her, recapturing her
mouth in the middle of Keely's laughter at his solution.

Not that she was any more willing to wait than he
was. Not when her blood was rushing through her
veins. Not when every part of her body was crying
out for him. Not when the knowledge that they would
be together forever took away all inhibitions and left
her feeling free to prove to him how she felt.

Jeans and T-shirt were discarded, and so was the
bridesmaid's dress and everything underneath it so
that Devon could leave no portion of her body unex-
plored even as he writhed beneath the searching,
seeking hands that were doing the same to him.

Tongues plundered and played, teased and tor-
mented and then parted so mouths could do some
magic on other, more intimate spots until need grew
so strong in them both that neither of them could hold
back any longer.

Devon slipped inside her as if he'd found his home
and together they made wild, unfettered love as if the
unquenched desires of that last morning they'd been
together had merely gained steam ever since. Now it
released its pent-up power, its potency, driving them
to the ultimate crest where they each found a climax

so explosive Keely wondered if sparks actually might have shot up from behind that sofa for anyone passing by to see through the picture window.

And when it was over and they were spent and exhausted and lying in each other's arms, Devon pressed his brow to the top of her head and said, "I love you, Keely."

"I love you, too. So much."

"So much you'll marry me and be patient if my domestication takes a little time?"

That made her smile against the broad chest she was using as a pillow. "Your *domestication?*"

"Mmm. Husband. Father. Those are pretty domesticated things."

Keely made a show of looking at where they were. "I don't know. I doubt there will ever stop being a wild streak in you."

"Probably not completely. But are you okay with that?"

"I'm okay with a happy medium."

He smiled down at her. "That's what I thought about you—that you're the best of both worlds—practical, pragmatic, down-to-earth, responsible, respectable. Until I get you in the bedroom—or on the living-room floor—and then…"

"Complaints?"

"Oh no," he said, squeezing her tight. "In fact if you give me a little nap, I think we might even be able to do this again before Mishka brings Harley home."

"By all means, sleep then," Keely said.

He kissed her again, a long, slow, deep kiss. Then he settled back with a replete sigh as Keely closed her eyes, too.

But she wasn't weary enough to sleep. She just wanted to savor being in his arms, knowing that from then on it was something she could have whenever she wanted. For the rest of her life.

Knowing, too, that before long Harley would be back and she could truly claim the baby as her very own.

And that finally she would have all her dreams come true.

* * * * *

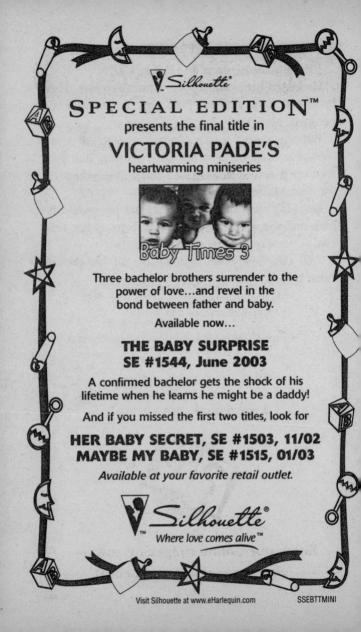

From *USA TODAY* bestselling author

EMILIE RICHARDS

**comes the story of a woman who has played life
by the book, and now the rules have changed.**

Faith Bronson, daughter of a prominent Virginia senator and wife
of a charismatic lobbyist, finds her privileged life shattered when
her marriage ends abruptly. Only just beginning to face the lie
she has lived, she finds sanctuary with her two children in a
run-down row house in exclusive Georgetown. This historic
house harbors deep secrets of its own, secrets that force Faith
to confront the deceit that has long defined her.

PROSPECT STREET

"Richards adds to the territory
staked out by such authors as
Barbara Delinsky and Kristin Hannah....
Richards' writing is unpretentious and
effective and her characters burst with
vitality and authenticity."

—*Publishers Weekly*

*Available the first week of June 2003
wherever paperbacks are sold!*

MIRA®

MER693